LANDING

LANDING

LAIA FÀBREGAS

Translated from the Spanish by
Samantha Schnee

Hispabooks Publishing, S. L.
Madrid, Spain
www.hispabooks.com

Originally published in Spain as *Landen* by Alfaguara, 2011
First published in English by Hispabooks, 2016

ISBN 978-84-944262-5-4 (trade paperback)
ISBN 978-84-944262-6-1 (ebook)
Legal Deposit: M-23492-2016

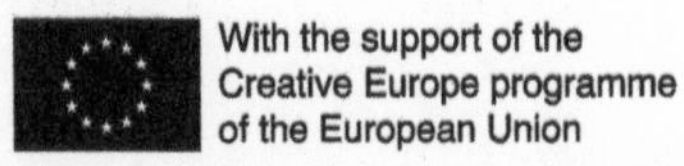

The European Commission support for the production of this publication does not constitute an endorsement of the contents which reflects the views only of the authors, and the Commission cannot be held responsible for any use which may be made of the information contained therein.

Her

He died while we were landing.

During take-off I had noticed how his hands were riveted to his knees and how the veins beneath his skin seemed to be thickening. I hoped he wasn't in pain. As soon as we were airborne, he relaxed. The cabin lights shone brightly. Although I normally wouldn't, I talked to him. I asked him if he was afraid of flying. He said that he hadn't flown in ten years.

He was on his way to visit his eldest son.

"My Dutch son," he said under his breath.

His speech was broken, as he searched for words in an invisible dictionary that seemed like it hadn't been cracked in years. His sentences unspooled like snippets of a poem with an unusual rhythm. Although all three of his sons had been born in the Netherlands, he said with pride, only the eldest was truly Dutch. It was as though the latter two had received more Spanish genes than the first, Arjen. Perhaps the choice of his name had influenced his future from the very start. If they had named him Simon or Robert, like the other two, he never would have had to spell out his name in Spain, and he would have felt much more at home in his father's country. But no. They named him Arjen and now, forty-four years later, his home was in Amsterdam, whereas his brothers lived in Barcelona.

He spoke to me as if we had known each other a long time. There was a familiarity about his demeanor, which was both appealing and discomfiting. Without my prompting him, he offered that he'd been born in a town somewhere in the heart of Spain. In the sixties he'd emigrated to Holland for work. Initially it wasn't easy for him to pick up Dutch, but then he met a remarkable woman; he knew he wanted to marry her, and that he'd have to learn her language.

He paused briefly, savoring the memory for a moment.

The cabin crew passed by with the bar cart. He opened his tray-table and asked what there was to eat. I told him that airplane food was no longer free, and he looked at me incredulously. I showed him the menu, and he realized he didn't want anything after all. He whispered that he would just be eating to keep himself busy; he said that I was also keeping him busy by listening to his stories, and he continued his tale.

For ten years he had been the happiest man in the world, he said. Holland was a good place to live and the summers in Spain were hot, a time to focus on family. Until his wife became ill. At first they didn't know what was wrong. Eventually the doctors said that a warmer climate would help. The boys were between the ages of six and eleven when, in the seventies, they filled the car with their belongings and moved to a town north of Barcelona.

He was silent for a moment, gazing at me. I looked at him: those eyes that had once been dark brown were now light gray, brimming with experience. I realized I almost never spoke with old people, and that I almost never sat next to them. I couldn't recall the last time I had looked at, and admired, an elderly person.

He said that it had been so long since he'd been to Holland that his Dutch had gotten rusty. He said this as though I wouldn't have noticed. I told him that he spoke Dutch very well, and he swelled with pride.

He had put a wooden box down on the seat between us. He had brought it to show his eldest son.

Then I plugged in my iPod and went to sleep. When I woke up, the pilot was announcing that we had begun our descent. I turned off the music. My seatmate became agitated again. His hands clutched his knees, as they had during takeoff. I looked at him once more, he smiled at me, and I silently wished him a happy landing before looking out the window at the landscape slipping past.

When the wheels touched down on the asphalt I felt an angel sigh in my ear.

The vehicle came to a halt and everyone on the plane began preparing to get up, putting on jackets, reaching for their luggage. His body remained in the same position, his hands glued to his knees and his head leaning slightly forward. I looked at his face, touched his shoulder, and felt my heart shrink.

We were united in silence, people bustling all around us. I knew that everyone had arrived home safely, except him, and I felt alone. Much more alone than usual. We were in row twenty-two. Soon there was no one left on the plane and a stewardess began to check the seats. She did it with confidence that the plane was empty. I wasn't sure whether I wanted her attention, or if I wanted more time to say good-bye. To make myself invisible I shrank down in my seat. I looked at the man and tried to remember everything he had told me. Maybe there was a son, a daughter-in-law, and some grandchildren waiting for him in the arrivals hall. I was overcome with guilt: I had become the person who had heard the last words of their father and grandfather.

The stewardess was startled when she saw us. She asked me why we had not left the aircraft.

"He's not moving."

"What do you mean?"

"I think he's dead."

The stewardess moved her hand toward the man's head, but an unseen force prevented her from touching his body. Instead, she moved her hand above his head, toward the panel beneath the overhead luggage compartment. She pressed the red button over and over again nervously.

"How long has he been dead?"

"I think he died while we were landing."

The stewardess kept staring down the aisle.

"I'm going to get some help. Would you stay here a moment?" she asked, wavering. I nodded.

She walked away and I suddenly felt like I needed air. I got up, leaned forward, and tried to get out of my seat. I pressed the button on his armrest and pushed the back of his chair. That gave me a little more space to climb over his legs. I grabbed my bag and the newspaper I had bought at the airport in Barcelona and lifted one leg over him. I leaned momentarily against the seat back of the chair in front until the toes of my right foot touched the floor of the aisle. I quickly lifted my left leg and shifted all my weight with a little hop. I nearly fell into the seats on the other side of the aisle, but at least I hadn't had to move the man, and I hadn't bumped him accidentally, which is what I had been most afraid of.

I looked at his face from the other side. He looked like a different person. I didn't even know his name. I only knew the name of his dead wife, Willemien. And those of his sons, Arjen, Simon, and Robert.

I noticed the box again, still lying on the middle seat. I grabbed it. Then I removed my small suitcase from the luggage compartment and put the box inside it.

In the other compartment I found the man's jacket and a suitcase. I left his luggage on the seat in front of him. I resisted the impulse to touch his shoulder once more, I promised him that I would take good care of his box, and I left. On the gangway I ran into the stewardess, who was approaching the plane with two uniformed men. I told them I didn't know the passenger and that I was in a hurry.

"I think you need to stay until the police arrive," the younger of the two men stammered, while his eyes appealed to his colleague for support.

"Why?" I asked. Apparently it was a difficult question. The men looked at each other until the older one said:

"Know what? Give us your phone number and if the police have any questions they can call you."

I gave them Ana Mei Balau's business card and left. I took the train home. Outside everything was dark and silent, flat and orderly. Inside it was full of people who had been to work and were returning home on a regular old Monday. I found an empty seat in front of two girls who were chatting. I always tried to sit next to loved-up couples or chatty girls. I was silent all the way home, no one tried to engage me in conversation. That day I also decided that from then on I'd always sit near young people. I didn't want to experience someone dying next to me ever again.

In Centraal Station it took me a while to find my bicycle in the crowded bike parking area. I tied my suitcase to the luggage rack and pedaled down Haarlemmerdijk. I stopped in front of The Movies, bought a ticket for a Japanese film, and entered the cinema.

That night I got home earlier than usual, it wasn't even midnight. I left my suitcase outside my room and got in bed, hoping the fatigue from the flight would help me fall asleep.

At six the alarm went off. Life was as dark and distant as ever, and in the street people were scraping ice off their windshields. After a freezing journey on my bicycle, at seven I was seated at my desk in the headquarters of the Dutch Tax Authority in Amsterdam.

Him

I don't like flying, I've never liked it, but choosing a new life in a foreign country makes it a necessity. Not just once, but every time you want to shorten the distance between past and present.

The days kept getting longer, full of silences and memories from other places. Willemien died just when I had gotten used to living without the boys, to being two instead of five, four, or three. All of a sudden I was one. The same year that Robert moved to Barcelona to work, Willemien died, and my reasons to remain in Figueres seemed to vanish. In the vacuum of Willemien's absence I began to discover little things around me. The nooks and crannies of the house, the organization of drawers of clothes, and sounds from the street began to intrude upon my consciousness with unfamiliar intensity. I realized that everything around me was irrevocably linked to Willemien. I hadn't heard the sounds from the street, or the upstairs neighbors' pipes, it was Willemien who had heard them, and who had made me sharpen my ears to hear them with her. I didn't know whether the walls of the hallway in our home were white or cream, it was Willemien who, when we were visiting friends, had pointed out that the walls in our hallway were darker than theirs.

Realizing this was what hurt the most. Reminded of her absence just by the sound of a truck unloading gas cylinders in the street, I kept withdrawing until finally I had to do something drastic.

I packed up the house. I put everything in one of the rooms that had a lock in order to be able to rent our place in Figueres without having to sell our things or take them with me. All my things.

That was when I came across the box I hadn't seen for so many years. It was locked, and though I searched high and low I couldn't find the key for its little iron lock. So, without opening it, I decided to take the box with me to my hometown, along with a small suitcase with some clothes and two books.

In the train, on the way home, I imagined that the box was full of sand from the beach Willemien and I had visited the first day we had gone to look at the sea. The day when I told her she was the most beautiful girl in Scheveningen and she began to laugh, because she never did know how to handle a compliment, or because I had mispronounced the name of the most famous beach in The Hague.

When I arrived in Holland I was confronted with one of the coldest winters in the country's history. People said such low temperatures hadn't been recorded in the past fifty years. It wasn't out of the ordinary for canals and lakes to completely freeze over, and to see the Dutch skating across them. But that year's winter was much harder, that year even the pipes froze, leaving us without running water. It was February 1963 and I had arrived to work for one year, after which I'd return home with the money, knowledge, and experience that living abroad gives you. That was my initial plan. A plan that had been a long time in the making.

Everything began in October 1962. I had spent the day working on the farm, beneath a satanic sun. My father and my brother had returned to the village earlier to stop at the blacksmith's house and fix some tools. Which is to say, that day I walked all the way home alone. When I was nearly there, I ran into the manager of the union office, who showed me a notice recently received from Madrid. It was from the Department of Labor, and it was about foreign businesses looking for workers. He asked me if I'd like to go to some faraway land to earn a lot of money fast, and I answered, without giving it a second thought, that I wasn't interested.

But the story didn't end there. He'd planted a seed, and day after day that adventure into the unknown, full of possibilities, beckoned. I'd leave for another country, where I'd earn loads of money in no time, I'd help my family without having to work the farm, and then I'd come home and build a house. And I'd be far from Mariana, the distance that was necessary to begin a new life. The past would be behind me.

Then I had a dream. I was in another country, working in a giant ship, with incredibly high ceilings and round skylights. I was building giant light bulbs out of pieces of thick glass, which fit together like the pieces of a puzzle and magically soldered themselves together. When I was finished, I had built an enormous light bulb, perfect and transparent. I stood there a moment looking at it and I realized I only needed to polish it for it to shine like the sun. So I did.

I was surrounded by light bulbs like mine, each one attended by a man. Each of us was looking after his light bulb the same way my father looked after the tools he used to work the land he rented for the farm. I remember being incredibly happy in the dream, a feeling of belonging like I felt at home, the same feeling I sometimes felt excluded from when I watched my father and my brother working side by side.

When I awoke I knew I had to leave.

I knew my father wouldn't like the idea. He had been upset when I had announced that I was going to work as a busboy at La Moraleja del Peral, in the Café de los Señores. But we all knew that work on the farm wasn't for me, that I wasn't suited to work on the farm. Ever since I can remember I've known that I'm a disappointment to my father. He had prepared me to be his successor, but I had slowly handed back the title he had looked after so carefully for me. Fortunately my brother Pedro was ready and willing to accept the position. And along with this position, he won my father's admiration as well.

I kept helping with the farm, but we all knew there was a clear line between helping and working. And then, when Mariana began to show up, bringing us lunch, I began to show up less and less. That's why I found the job at the Café de los Señores. And that's how Pedro won. He won it all, despite the fact that he never competed for a thing.

Despite the fact I was only helping on the farm, I still worried that they wouldn't be able to get on without me, because six hands are better than four. The girls, as we called my sisters back then, were much younger than us and still couldn't lend a hand.

I didn't say anything to anyone, but I went to the union office. They talked to me about Holland, they said I could work at Philips. It reminded me of the radio at the Café de los Señores, of the shining letters I read every day as "pilix." I imagined they built or polished these radios—which were still made of wood back then—and other futuristic devices, and added my name to the list, which already had four young men from the town.

The following day my father learned my name was on the list. He searched for me all over the village, found me in the bar, and asked me to step outside. Out on the main street, as we crossed the five meters that separated the door of the bar from the shade on the other side of the street, I prepared myself to receive a few heavy blows and the news that he had removed my name from the list.

But when we got to the other side of the street, when we were under cover from the harsh afternoon sun, he said I had his blessing. That it would be good for me to find work I was better suited to, and on which I could earn a living.

I was speechless. He went on to say that I should return when I had saved up enough money, and that I should write often, especially to my mother and the girls, who would miss me terribly. And so the unexpected came to pass.

Families can be unfathomable.

A few days later word arrived from the Spanish Institute of Emigration that I had to go to Cáceres for a medical exam. I went and I passed. In November I signed the contract and learned my first Dutch word: *Gloeilampenfabriek*. A word with twenty letters! A few months passed before I learned that my first Dutch word was actually three words:

gloei, lampen, and *fabriek.* Factory of incandescent lamps, light bulb factory.

In theory the group was supposed to leave for Holland in December but everything was postponed until February on account of the weather—a cold snap had paralyzed northern Europe. It was as if the country had put on such a frigid winter to prevent us Extremadurans from coming. But Holland didn't know that we, in addition to being quite stubborn, needed work as badly as we needed our daily bread, and in our unheated homes in Extremadura we were unfazed by the idea of meters of snow and frozen lakes. We weren't fazed at all, mostly because we had never seen such things, and we couldn't even imagine such cold. We would get to Holland, sooner or later.

The two-month delay was difficult. When you see yourself in another place, another life, it takes a lot of energy to carry on in the life you so badly want to leave behind. And around me, my family was preparing to take over the space I was going to vacate.

"When he's gone we'll do this, when he's gone we'll do that," my father said, day after day. It seemed that, instead of robbing them of my help on the farm, I was opening up a world of opportunities, which my brother and father would greatly enjoy.

The girls told me not to go, they'd miss me too much. My mother kept her silence, her eyes fixed on the horizon, and Pedro didn't say a word.

Sometimes, my worries about leaving turned into doubts and I wanted to stay, especially when I saw Mariana. When I saw her alone, at the market, talking to the woman who sold vegetables, or with her friends, walking down the high street. I'd imagine that everything that had transpired had not, and that I should stay and take her dancing the following Saturday.

But sometimes seeing her made me want to pack my bags and start walking to Cáceres, to wait there for whatever time was left, until the bus that would take me to the future arrived. Those were the days when I ran into her and she wasn't alone, when I saw her walking through the village hand in hand with Pedro. That was the sight that pained me most, because it was inexorable proof that all was lost.

Her

"How was your trip?"

I knew someone would ask me the question, and I had even prepared a few polite, innocuous replies, but when I heard the question all I could think was *What does it matter to you?*

"Great," I heard myself say, thinking of the dead man.

"Nice weather in my favorite city?"

Favorite city. It irritated me when people used such expressions. I stared at my computer screen, ready to snap back, *Who cares about the weather! What do you want to hear, that the weather was good, or not?*

"Great," I repeated.

"Of course it was, the weather's always nice in Barcelona."

From the way he said it, it was clear he'd said it many times before.

"I bet you're tired from the trip and everything you saw there . . . I'll leave you alone, you can tell me about your adventures some other time."

I wondered why people don't give up. Why at the beginning of the week everyone asks me how my weekend was, and what exactly they expected me to say. I could have given an honest answer, like *It was a total disaster, I spent my Saturday searching, calling, and asking all around town, and I still haven't found a thing.* Or *I'm dead-tired, I need another day off because I spent the weekend trying to put my life back together.* Or *I made a quick trip to and from Groningen for a brief, pointless meeting, and when I got home I saw I had a missed call from an unidentified number. And I've spent all day wondering whether or not that call was* the call.

How can you tell someone something like that? How could I really tell them what I did outside of the office? It was simply impossible.

That morning after the trip was one of those days when I had to face the reality of office life, with its obligations of collegiality and the need for departmental harmony. That morning I told myself for the millionth time that it wasn't their fault, they were just being sociable, and that I had to learn to put up with it. If not, I'd be back in my boss's office for our usual conversation:

"Your work is impeccable, excellent, but you know that for us teamwork is really important.

"Yes, I know."

"You have to be a little more sociable, it's important for the team."

"I'll try."

And we'd both understand that everything, apart from the excellence of my work, was a lie.

But I had to try to fit in better, I couldn't run the risk of them getting rid of me, because I was in the perfect position, with the authorizations I needed, to be able to continue my search.

Since I felt I was being watched that day, I didn't search the databases. Around five in the afternoon I was tempted to type one of the names on my list into the search field, but in the end I resisted.

I survived that day. After work I went to Karen Abrams's bar for dinner.

Karen Abrams was the first person I found. Two years prior I had entered her bar sweating from the long bicycle trip, my stomach cramping from nerves. But Karen Abrams turned out to be an easy one.

She had listened to me attentively, she was behind the bar when I began talking to her and she understood that my story was important. She put her hand on my arm and said,

"We should talk about this somewhere else."

Immediately, I thought she knew something. My heart jumped and my knees trembled. She noticed.

"I don't think I can help you," she quickly added. "But if we can talk quietly perhaps I'll be able to help you some day."

She shouted to the kitchen for someone to fill in for her behind the bar, and we climbed the stairs to her apartment, one floor up. It was lighter in her dining room, she looked younger and prettier. That's when I realized it couldn't have been her.

The open kitchen was separated from the dining room by a bar counter which reminded me of the one downstairs. As if she spent the morning practicing to be the best barkeep she could be in the afternoons. She poured a cup of tea and I sat down at the table.

When she sat down opposite me I saw she was a natural blonde, her face was drawn and fragile, like the rest of her body. Her fingers wrapped around her teacup, long and thin. She exuded kindness and peace, but when I saw she was waiting I didn't know where to begin. I hesitated; I still hadn't shown my list to anyone. She continued looking at me and I told myself there was nothing to fear. I took the paper out of my wallet and unfolded it. My hands were shaking. I turned the list and slid it toward her. She placed a finger carefully on each corner of the paper. She read all the names. After a few minutes' silence she lifted her gaze toward me.

"I'm the first," she asked, with a touch of pride.

"You?"

"Me, well I don't know, it could be me or someone else with the same name, no?"

"It's in alphabetical order."

"So I see."

She started to push the list back toward me, but paused.

"What would happen if I were?"

"If you were what?"

"If I were *that* Karen Abrams."

"You might be."

"So what am I doing with all those people? What do we have in common that puts us on the list?"

"In all likelihood it's not you. It's probably some other Karen Abrams it's referring to."

"What makes you so sure?"

"Have you ever been to Someren?"

"No."

"That's what I thought. Then it can't be you."

"Why Someren?"

She was kind, but she was getting on my nerves, she was too interested in becoming part of my search.

"Do you want to help me?" I asked her while she smoothed the page with her fingers.

"I'd like to try."

"Next Saturday I'll stop by with the addresses of all the other Karen Abramses. Maybe you can search through them."

That day I left wondering whether I had told her too much. In time I learned not to disclose everything to the people I found. The reason for my search would only interest the person I was looking for.

Two years later, when I entered her bar after the trip to Barcelona, Karen Abrams still hadn't done what I had asked her to do that day, but it no longer mattered. I had found in her a silent accomplice, someone who knew what I was trying to achieve.

"How was your trip?" she asked when I walked in. This time I knew what she meant by her question.

"No new news," I said calmly. "But a lot happened."

"Tell me. Did you find Ana Mei Balau?" she asked with an empty glass in one hand, the other on the beer tap.

"Yeah, I finally talked to her, but she's not the one."

"Bummer." The beer settled in the glass.

"She didn't know anything, but she said she wanted to help me. Though I don't think she can."

She passed me the beer she had just poured. I wanted to tell Karen Abrams about the man who had died without telling me his name, but she didn't give me a chance.

"You should focus on Holland, I'm sure you won't find anything abroad. Dead sure. And I'm saying that because I care about you, sweetie. I want you to find what you're looking for with all my heart! So forget about planes; take your train and your bike, everything you need is here, in our little country."

She had no idea what she was saying. She liked to play the wise one and I let her. The bar was practically my second home.

"Do you have time for dinner tonight? I'd like to tell you the good news from my trip."

She agreed. It was strange to call it good news, when it was about a dead man with no name. I just wanted to tell her about the box.

After dinner I got on my bike and looked to see if there was anything I hadn't seen yet playing at The Movies, but there wasn't. I pedaled slowly and impatiently home. I still had three hours to kill before I'd feel tired enough to sleep, and I knew from experience I couldn't spend more than two hours at home awake and alone.

Him

On February 5, 1963, the bus that was picking up those of us from Extremadura who had been contracted to work for Philips passed through village after village on its way to Cáceres. The bus was already half-full when it stopped on the high street; three young men boarded with me. It was a difficult good-bye. Along with my parents and the girls, Pedro and Mariana had showed up to wish me a safe trip. I gave Pedro a hug and told him I'd continue to help out, wherever I was, if not with my hands then with my money. I left with one small suitcase. I gave Mariana two final kisses, one on each cheek, and boarded the bus. I felt her cheeks against mine for hours afterwards.

In Cáceres we boarded a train to Madrid. There were ninety of us and we were slowly getting to know one another. We spoke excitedly about what we would find and how we had come this far. I also heard lots of stories about those who had wanted to join us but stayed behind.

I felt fortunate to be there.

In Madrid they put us up in a hotel, which seemed beyond luxurious to us. It was like being back in my dream with the gigantic light bulbs.

On February 6 the train for Holland left Madrid. Two coaches had been reserved for us, including a restaurant car. We felt very important; we were going to help the Dutch, who had employed us and sent a train to collect us, despite the fact they wouldn't be able to understand a word we said. By that time many of us had already forgotten the sorrow of our departure, thinking only of the adventure awaiting us.

We traveled through Irún and then Paris, and the train finally deposited us in Roosendaal. When we set foot on Dutch soil it wasn't soil, but frozen water. My shoes sank into the centimeters-thick snow that lay everywhere, blanketing everything within sight.

From Roosendaal they sent us by bus to Someren, a town twenty kilometers south of Eindhoven. On the outskirts of Someren there was a development that had been built in the thirties to house workers who were draining the marshes. The development, with its little wooden houses, not unlike the bungalows you see in campgrounds today, would be our new home. I would share a bedroom and a living room with seven other young men.

The morning after we arrived a bus was waiting to take us to the Philips factory. I still remember clearly that feeling of entering a brand new world. I had never worked in a factory, or in any large business; I knew only the farm and the Café de los Señores. The Philips factory was different. It was a space that breathed teamwork, the organization and cooperation that made it possible for parts to enter one end and machines to come out the other, on a journey that was supervised and assisted by hundreds of conscientious hands engaged in the same mission.

At the factory we were met by a Spaniard who worked as an interpreter. He explained that we had to pass a few tests to be able to operate the machines. After two days of evaluations, tired of so many tests, all we could think about was doing something useful, finally getting to work.

The first day of work eventually arrived, but the long-awaited moment was a disappointment for me; instead of radios or televisions, instead of cables and bulbs, they gave me a broom. A broom for sweeping. Sweeping! My job was cleaning the floors of the factories and offices! In my contract it specifically stated "specialized laborer". How dare they set a specialized laborer to work cleaning? Where were my gigantic light bulbs? I had never swept a floor in my life. That was woman's work. What about my devotion to building the best light bulb in the world?

That first day I spent the morning reluctantly cleaning floors and sweeping up dust. In the afternoon I remembered that in my dream, after building the light bulb, I cleaned it, and I found a glimmer of hope in this. I calmed down a little, after all, perhaps this had been part of my dream: I was cleaning in the light bulb factory. The time to build the giant light bulb would come. I was sure of it. I just needed to be patient, and do my job well.

But though I told myself over and over that I should wait patiently and everything would change, I felt completely out of place that first week. I missed real work, even the livestock and the hard physical labor of the farm. I had travelled two thousand kilometers just to clean floors in a sunless country.

One night I had a nightmare in which Mariana saw me with the broom in my hands and began laughing hysterically. She laughed so hard she cried. It was awful waking up with that image in my head. That day I regretted putting my name on the union's list.

The only consolation was knowing I wasn't alone in my disgrace, that I wasn't the only one who had been handed a broom. We took as much pride in our clean floors as those who'd had better luck and were working with radios and televisions, and they didn't make fun of us. They tried to cheer us up, telling us we'd soon have better jobs, and that their jobs weren't as great as we thought.

I immediately signed up for the Dutch classes they offered Saturday afternoons and poured all my energy into learning the language. I figured that if they weren't going to let me touch the machines I'd have to develop other skills if I wanted to change jobs.

I learned Dutch very slowly, but I learned it. Most of my compatriots went to class once and never returned. They felt no need to learn the language because the company had made interpreters available to us everywhere we went: in the camp, in the human resources department, even the department managers were required to communicate with us in Spanish. And then there was the fact we had all set out on this adventure thinking it would last one year, and you couldn't learn a language in one year alone, or so they said. My contract was for one year, too, but I must have known even then that I would stay longer.

The job with the broom helped me focus on learning Dutch. If I had been operating machines I would have had to focus intently on my job, but since my work was simple—basically making piles of dust—I could work with my hands while my head was busy memorizing the vocabulary from my latest Dutch class.

Twice a week I cleaned the offices of the administrators, who were all Dutch. Unlike the first few days, when I would lower my head in shame when I entered those offices, once

I began to stammer my first few words of Dutch I wanted to be among those tables, writing desks, and telephones. I'd enter an office and would surprise everyone with a well-rehearsed "jude-morge," especially the women, who would smile at me and reply *goede morgen*, articulating each syllable. In the beginning I stuck to "good morning." But then I'd try out new phrases, and each week they would reply with a few more words. Some words I recognized, some I didn't, and I did my best to remember them until I left the offices, when I wrote them on a piece of paper, to save them for the next Saturday's Dutch class.

One day, as I was passing through the offices with my broom and my rag and my newly acquired words, I ran into one of the translators. I had already seen Miguel on several occasions, when he came to the camp with the company journalist, who sometimes interviewed us for his column in the *Philips Koerier*. But I had never spoken to him. Miguel was surprised by my small talk with the secretaries, and from that day forward he would stop to speak with me when we saw each other in the factory or the camp, teaching me new words.

After a few weeks the inevitable came to pass, and the Saturday Dutch classes were canceled. My compatriots preferred to play soccer on teams improvised from the camps or go to the bar in lieu of studying. But I stuck to my plans to learn the language, one way or another. So the next time I saw Miguel, without hesitating, I asked him to give me one-on-one lessons. I told him I couldn't afford to pay him much and he said I didn't have to pay him a thing.

From then on we met occasionally after work; we'd walk through town and he'd speak Dutch to me. If it was really cold, or if we felt like sitting, we'd go to a bar and continue the class there. I learned many words from Miguel, and it was through him that I met Willemien.

Looking back, it might seem that my goal in life was to be the third wheel.

Willemien was leaning against a motorbike, talking to another girl in front of the bar. She was pale blonde and although the weather was still as frigid as it had been the day I arrived, she was wearing a knee-length skirt and high heels with buckles.

Miguel and I had headed to the bar to warm up after freezing our feet wandering through the end-of-March carpet of snow.

The girl that was talking to Willemien said good-bye and rode off on her bike. When the girl turned to wave good-bye to her friend I thought she'd wipe out as she turned the corner, but the girl handled her bike like Bahamontes himself.

Willemien was left standing alone by the motorbike, like she was waiting for someone. The image of her silhouette and her smile were burned into my memory forevermore. I thought of speaking to her, of approaching her and starting a conversation, just as I had done with many other girls in recent years. But then I realized I couldn't make conversation, all I had were words and phrases, and a terrible fear that she'd laugh at me.

Miguel, however, could start a conversation, and, naturally, he approached Willemien. His stride was quick and confident, and I saw her smile, inviting him to speak to her, just as I wanted to. I hung back, eager to learn how to win over a woman in Dutch. But I was shocked to see they didn't exchange a single word. He stroked her cheek with his hand, which he then wrapped around the back of her neck, and moved his lips toward hers, kissing her briefly but decisively.

Lifetimes have passed since that moment, but I still don't like saying that my beloved Willemien, my wife and companion throughout so many years, joys, and sorrows, was Miguel's girlfriend back then. Miguel, the translator who combined the charm of being Spanish, as was I, with the intelligence and resourcefulness of being able to say everything he wanted in Willemien's language, something I was light years away from being able to do.

Summer arrived without us even noticing. Suddenly it was June and then July, but the temperature didn't shoot up, the sun didn't burn, the nights were still cold. Whereas Dutch people's faces turned pink from the few rays of sun that managed to break through the clouds, ours grew paler by the day.

At the end of July there were a few stifling days, which reminded us of our warmer summers. And it was on one of those days that we heard the good news that Philips had organized a holiday back home for us.

On August 9, 1963 we boarded two buses, which would take us to Extremadura for eight days of vacation.

We arrived in town at night. A crowd awaited us in the plaza. My mother and the girls were there, they had grown so much in half a year that Antonia, the eldest, was now a young woman. The first thing she asked when she saw me, before even giving me a hug, was whether I had a girlfriend yet.

I told her I did. That her name was Willemien and that she was very pretty. Antonia was silent for a moment, then she asked, "And will she come and live with us?"

"Of course she will, next year I'll bring her with me." Maria and Celia, the little ones, laughed timidly.

My mother embraced me and thanked me for all the money I had been sending. We walked home while the girls peppered me with questions, not even giving me time to answer.

When we arrived, Pedro and my father weren't home and Mariana was making dinner. Antonia entered first, shouting that her big brother had a Dutch girlfriend. Mariana came into the dining room, her hands still bloodied by the chicken she had just killed. She smiled and congratulated me, and I realized things had changed while I had been in Holland. Everything was the same, but everything was different.

They had changed the bedrooms around. Antonia now slept in my old room, so Maria and Celia no longer had to share a bed. My mother told me to sleep in the living room, on the new sofa they had bought with the money I had sent them.

I didn't tell them that in Someren I had seven roommates. The sofa in the living room would be just fine.

Over dinner I told them stories about light bulbs and televisions, about the cold, the snow, and the green spring. Antonia learned to say *goe-de-mor-gen* while Pedro and my father watched me, wondering who was this man who had showed up unannounced for dinner.

The next morning I went with my father to the farm to lend him a hand. The sun burned my skin, and walking along unpaved roads I felt my feet truly touched the ground. My father walked ahead of me, silent. I talked to him about what we would do with all the money I had saved, the following year when I returned. We'd buy a car, we'd build a house for me and Willemien, and another one for Pedro and Mariana. My father agreed to everything as though it made no difference, and that's when I realized I wouldn't return the following year.

That was the shortest and strangest summer of my life. I enjoyed sweating beneath the sun. I enjoyed the afternoon siestas and the midnight conversations in the town plaza. I told lies full of light bulbs, while the other "Dutchmen" in town invented their own jobs, full of danger and excitement. We were selling illusions. I'm certain that summer we convinced more than a few people to come and join us in our new country at the first chance they got.

On the way back to Holland on the Philips bus, I pondered how to finally approach Willemien.

Returning to the routine with my broom, meals, and life in the camp in Someren was harder than I had expected. The week at home had brought my fragile command of Dutch to a screeching halt, and fall was already starting. Afternoons were gray and the days grew rapidly shorter. September was a difficult month.

But then everything changed. In early October the boss called me in to offer me a position in the television department; I was flabbergasted. Despite the fact it was the news I had been waiting for since the day I came to terms with my broom, the first thought that crossed my mind when I imaged myself building televisions was that I'd miss my conversations in Dutch with the people in the admin department. My plan had been to spend a year cleaning, after which I'd request a job translating, and on that day, when I'd go to work as a cleaner and return home as a translator, my life would change completely, because I would have caught up with Miguel.

That's why I looked at the boss and asked slowly, choosing my words carefully, if there were other options. The man looked at me incredulously, and asked me what other options I thought there were. I realized my Dutch still wasn't good enough, that my little dream of becoming a translator wasn't based on reality, and I told him that I'd accept the transfer to televisions.

The day I began to put together cathode tubes was the day I didn't have to lie in my letters home any longer.

Her

"Why don't you try to find the son who was waiting for the dead man at the airport?" Karen Abrams asked while I looked at the menu, only to order the same thing as ever.

"Why?"

"Maybe he could tell you something about what's in the box."

"And how am I going to find him?"

"You don't know his last name, right?"

"No."

"But you know his name is Arjen and that his surname is Spanish, yeah?"

"Yeah?"

"Never mind."

Karen Abrams always had these kinds of ideas, they seemed good at first but were pie in the sky. Then she'd go back and try to figure out a way to make them work, in some other place or time.

"If I were you," she said, "I would have looked for him at the airport, when he was waiting for his father."

"Yeah, it was a mistake not to look for him," I lied, "I just had to leave."

I had decided to open the box, and we didn't need the son for that. And in truth, I didn't need the box either, I had enough work with my hundred people, I couldn't handle another search on top of that. I'd never finish either of them.

That evening I didn't last long in Karen Abrams's bar. On the way home I called Anneke, to let her know everything was fine. Although sometimes I didn't, I had agreed to call Anneke whenever I was going away for a few days, and again when I got home.

It was always difficult for me to dial her number, but once we were speaking most of the time it was alright. Once in a while Jan answered the phone, and then it was easier. Jan didn't speak to me like a father. He never had.

Obviously they didn't know about my list, so I always had to make up an excuse for my trips. This time I said I had taken a long weekend to take a break from my grueling job.

Over the years Anneke had learned not to ask me too many questions, she knew that I would tell her only as much as I wanted to.

After our brief conversation I felt empty, but proud of having kept my promise.

On the way home I pondered what it would be like if all my conversations with Anneke were different, if I told her more. After all, I could have told her about Ana Mei Balau.

Jan used to say that the best jobs were the ones nobody knew about. I had never really understood what he meant until I met Ana Mei Balau. If Jan had picked up the phone that day, I would have told him about her.

Ana Mei Balau made an impression on me. My conversation with her didn't help my investigation, but she realized I had traveled a long way to meet her so she didn't kick me out. We started talking and she told me how she spent her days. She spoke nine languages: Dutch, English, Spanish, Catalan, French, Italian, German, Norwegian, and

Danish. I was impressed, but it was even more impressive how she used her command of these languages.

"I discover untranslatable words," she had said.

"What?"

"I look for words that exist in one language and not in another. Like the excellent Dutch word *gezellig.* Maybe it sounds clichéd, but it truly is a unique word."

"Yes, it does seem difficult to translate."

"But not for much longer."

My face said it all, I think, because I didn't have to ask her to explain what she meant, she just carried on.

"When I come across an untranslatable word, like *gezellig,* I study its symbolism and etymology. That helps me to determine the essence of the word. And that knowledge helps me invent an equivalent in the languages that don't have it."

She gave me a moment to absorb what she had just said, or perhaps she was expecting me to ask another question, but nothing occurred to me. She continued her explanation.

"I work for several European linguistic organizations, which pay me for every word I invent. Then I receive a royalty every time that word is used in print for the first few years it's in circulation."

I asked her to give me an example for the word *gezellig,* but she said that was confidential.

"All I have are authorial rights," she said apologetically. "I could tell you the English translation of *gezellig* but then if you use it in conversation I can't charge a penny. Because the word would exist before I register it, and it would no longer be considered my invention."

"The words you invent belong to you?"

"Yes, until I sell the copyright. No one knows I'm the one who invented them."

"Don't you think it's sad that your work goes unrecognized?"

"No. I know it's my work and every time I hear or read one of my words I'm happy. Plus I don't like being the center of attention."

"Can you tell me one of the words you've sold?"

"It's also in my contract that I can't publicize which words I've invented."

I looked around her apartment, at the art on the walls, the books on the side table, for a clue to a new word. But I didn't know what to look for.

Ana Mei Balau had seemed so mysterious that, on my way home in Amsterdam, as the first few drops of rain fell on my shoulders, I wondered whether she had been putting me on. There was no proof whatsoever that anything she had told me was true. All I could do was wait a few years until, during a trip to England or Germany, I heard a word for *gezellig* in English or German.

Back home, for once I went to bed early, hoping I wouldn't toss and turn for too long before falling asleep. By two a.m. I gave up. Going to bed early didn't help. I got up, like I did whenever a nightmare awoke me in the middle of the night. I walked around the house in the moonlight. I was always looking for something on these walks. Sometimes I found a book I had left out; I'd put it away and get back in bed. Sometimes I found the bathroom door open; I'd shut it and feel sleepy. It worked like a charm.

That night I walked from the bedroom through the hall to the other bedroom, the kitchen, the living room. I turned on the lights and sat down at the table. Slowly my eyes grew accustomed to the brightness. I looked around me. The suitcase from my trip to Barcelona was still outside the door to my bedroom. That's where it belonged, waiting for the next trip. I never unpacked my suitcase. The clothes and the toiletry bag inside could stay there for weeks on end, until I planned a new trip and repacked it.

A few years ago I had met a guy who did the same with his suitcases. His parents had split up when he was just a kid, and he had always lived between two homes. He said his suitcase was his real home, his father's house and his mother's were just extras. He never unpacked his suitcase. He assumed that my parents had gotten divorced too, and I let him believe it.

I looked at my suitcase and remembered that inside that red plastic shell there was more than just my clothes and my toiletry kit. There was also something I had borrowed. You might say I had stolen it, but I was certain the dead man knew I had only borrowed it. Some things go without saying. Some things you see and feel. My impulse to take the box had come from the dead man.

It was late and the living room was cold. I got up, went over to the suitcase, and opened it on the floor. I took the box out and noticed how my clothes held the shape of an invisible box. Before shutting the suitcase again I grabbed a pair of black socks. I went back to the table with the box and the socks. I sat down, put the box on the table, and put the socks on my chilly feet.

The box looked smaller now than it had on the airplane seat. It was about the same size as a jewelery box. Although it was painted black, on the corners you could see it was made of light-colored wood. I laid my hand on the lid and tried to sense what could be inside. I still couldn't tell. My fingers wandered over the cold lock on the front of the box.

Something had been left hanging in my conversation with the man: it was an unfinished dialogue; I hadn't told him my story. Perhaps I felt I needed to give something back because I had taken the box. And I felt certain that now he could tell what I was thinking, he could see what I was doing and expected me to share a bit of my life with him, just as he had shared a bit of his with me.

The next day I went to a locksmith. There was a small shop in my neighborhood that I always peered into when I passed by. Sometimes there was an old man inside, sometimes a younger man. No doubt they were father and son; they had the same nose. The shop was stuffed with things. The shelves along each wall served both for display and storage. In addition to making copies of keys and selling locks, they also refilled ink cartridges for printers, unblocked mobile phones, and sold hands-free kits for cars. Despite the chaos, it gave the impression of organization and harmony.

When I entered the shop that day, the young man was alone. He took the box and quickly opened the lock with a screwdriver. He lifted the lid half a centimeter and I put my hand on top of his to stop him. It was the wrong time and the wrong place. I said thanks and told him that was all I needed. He insisted upon installing a new lock. But I didn't want the box to remain in his hands a moment longer.

"I'll come back another day to put a new lock on," I lied. I took the box and walked out the shop.

At home I sat down on the sofa with the box in my lap. I didn't dare lift the lid. I was about to learn the secret I had stolen from a dead Spaniard. Looking at it that way, it didn't seem right.

The lid opened without a sound.

Him

October arrived, the Dutch winter with it. With the cold, my linguistic walks with Miguel tended to end more frequently in the bar, where they usually segued into a round of beers. One day, when I had already said good-bye to Miguel and was about to leave, Willemien walked into the bar. Out of the blue Miguel surprised me by asking me to stick around. All three of us could have a drink together. I agreed and greeted Willemien in her language with a broken and awkward "pleased to meet you," and she replied in Spanish.

I was so relieved that I spent the afternoon saying stupid things just to make her laugh. And she laughed, she laughed so much that Miguel couldn't hide his jealously beneath his neatly combed bangs. Because Miguel was intelligent and well-educated, but he had no sense of humor at all. Willemien was more interested in my jokes than her boyfriend's boring stories. It was embarrassing. Of course I realized what was happening and I could have stopped it. But I didn't want to, I wanted to get the girl for once, despite the fact that someone else had found her first. If she realized she had made a mistake, why not fix it? Something told me that a Dutch girl who spoke Spanish would fix it sooner than a girl from my hometown in Extremadura.

I saw that Miguel was getting angry at me, and at Willemien, but I didn't say anything. I saw how he kept his anger bottled up inside and how he stalked out resentfully, leaving his girlfriend alone with me; he didn't stop us. I realized I was losing my free Dutch lessons but I didn't make a move to stop him, because I knew I'd get something else instead.

Willemien asked Miguel why he was leaving, and he mumbled that he had things to do. She gave him a kiss on the cheek and went to the bar to order another round, just two glasses instead of three this time. I thought Miguel was a coward, that instead of giving up and leaving he should have lost his temper, slammed his fist on the table, and kicked me out of the bar. But he didn't. And now I know why. If Miguel had made a scene in the bar, Willemien would have smacked him in front of everybody, like she did once when I was acting cocky.

When we parted that night in October, Willemien told me we'd see each other again the following week, but not to try to reach her before that. I spent the week whistling among my televisions, and trying to avoid Miguel. After a week and a day, Willemien came to find me at the camp. She had broken up with Miguel. I didn't speak to him again for a year.

In mid-December they told us that Mr. Philips was giving us Christmas holidays. But this time they didn't send us to Spain, as they had in the summer. So I spent a few days wondering whether or not I should take the train home. And if I did, whether I would bring Willemien, or if it would be better to stay and celebrate my first Christmas in Holland. I decided to stay at the camp, like most of the guys.

It was my first Christmas in a country where the sun sets at four in the afternoon. I had been in Holland for nearly a year and little by little I was getting used to the climate, I was able to stammer a few words, but I still hadn't experienced how the Dutch celebrated the holiday so differently.

Holland had two days of Christmas: the 25th and the 26th of December; they called them "the first day of Christmas" and "the second day of Christmas." The ultimate manifestation of organization and consistency. At first it struck me as absurd. No one could explain to me why they had two days instead of one. Then I realized how sensible it was, to be able to celebrate Christmas without getting families together.

Christmas Eve was uneventful. Dinner was just like any other night and some of us attended midnight mass at the church in town. The next morning felt strange and cold; I remember awakening slowly, knowing it was Christmas but feeling like it wasn't really. We were lost in a dreamlike fog of indecision. In Holland there are many days when you don't see the sky. I remember that Christmas as the first day in my life that I realized I needed the sky.

After whiling away the morning, we put together the best Christmas dinner we could, convincing Peter, the cook, to let us dine on a Spanish schedule for once. He made us a meal that you couldn't call either Spanish or Dutch, but it was good, and we had fun, laughing and singing, and the day passed without us feeling homesick.

Some of us found it harder to enjoy the moment than others, because they missed their wives and children, who would be celebrating the festivities in Extremadura. I felt pretty good, because I had a girlfriend a few kilometers away, eating with her parents and eagerly awaiting the second day of Christmas, when we would see each other.

My first second day of Christmas in Holland was unquestionably a Dutch second day of Christmas. I had already met Willemien's parents several times, but they had never invited me to their house. It was a strange day. Instead of Christmas lunch, we had a Christmas dinner that began at five in the afternoon. And instead of everyone shouting across the table without understanding each other, most of the dinner took place in silence, broken only by the occasional question, which was answered curtly before silence resumed.

While I ate I imagined my parents, Pedro and Mariana, Antonia and the little ones, gathered around the dining room table at home, drinking coffee and shooting the breeze after Christmas lunch. They were about to clear the table and go for a walk, and I was just sitting down. Until I realized that they wouldn't be celebrating the second day of Christmas. They would be working and nostalgia made me miss them even more.

But I didn't miss them for long. The next day a letter from Pedro arrived, one I should have waited to open. I remember the words and the shapes of the letters clearly, I remember everything on that well-folded piece of paper, written in Mariana's hand, but signed with Pedro's name.

"Dear Brother. I'm going to marry Mariana. The wedding will be April 1. Your brother, Pedro."

It was neither an invitation to the wedding nor an announcement that I was not invited. It was notification of an event, which he knew I would not be able to attend. And it became the catalyst for my remaining in Holland.

On the last day of 1963 I asked Willemien to marry me. And she said yes.

Willemien's parents were clearly opposed to our engagement. Ever since "the Spaniards" had arrived in Someren all the families with young ladies had been on tenterhooks. Mothers rushed to find eligible Dutch candidates before their daughters showed up at home with Spaniards, and parents made disapproving faces when stories of the first romances reached their ears. Willemien knew very well that bringing a Spaniard home would lead to arguments with her parents, that's why she had never brought Miguel home, and as far as I know, they never even knew about him.

Willemien had wanted to go against her parents' wishes for years, and occasionally she succeeded. But she lost the battle on her education. Although she saw herself living in a dormitory in Maastricht, studying art at the Jan van Eyck Academie, her parents prevailed upon her to live at home and study textile design in Eindhoven. In the end she grudgingly agreed, but she took the first opportunity she had to sign up for art classes behind her parents' backs.

By the time I arrived on the scene things had calmed down; Willemien had graduated and was working as a clothing designer for local businesses. But my entrance into the family threatened to break the fragile peace. Willemien's parents never tried to hide their lack of enthusiasm for our relationship. No sooner had they learned of our intentions than they tried to delay the wedding as long as possible, hoping with all their hearts that their daughter would change her mind. One of their most compelling arguments against our union was that, by law, Willemien would lose her Dutch citizenship when we married.

Willemien couldn't have cared less, and sometimes she would say angrily that she would get married for better or for worse. But deep in her heart she craved her parents' approval, not to feel alone as she embarked on this unknown adventure of marriage to a foreigner.

Pedro and Mariana's wedding date approached, and Willemien and I still hadn't set a date. I hadn't told my family I was engaged, and I began to worry that we'd never get married when one Sunday morning a kid on a bicycle came to the camp shouting my name. I was playing cards with my roommates when I heard the boy. I looked out the window and saw a blond kid with long legs who couldn't have been more than ten. I had never seen him before. When I came out of the barracks wondering what he could possibly want from me, the boy approached me on his bike, stopping short in front of me, and handed me a piece of paper.

In Dutch it said, "We expect you for dinner at our house at five." It was an invitation from Willemien's parents. The boy stood looking at me and I wondered whether he was waiting for a tip or an answer. He snapped me out of it.

"Yes or no?" he asked expectantly.

"Yes."

I put the piece of paper in my pocket and returned to my card game. But I didn't win a single hand.

At four I left the camp for a leisurely three-kilometer walk to Willemien's house. I arrived at the specified hour, Willemien opened the door and I looked at her questioningly, expecting an explanation for this gathering, but I soon learned she knew as little as I did. She accompanied me to the living room and I noticed that the table was set for five. I wondered who the fifth person could be.

"Father Driessen is also coming," Willemien whispered in my ear.

Jaime Driessen was the Dutch priest who said mass in Spanish at all the guest-worker camps; he knew the first and last names and even the birthdays of every last one of us.

"Why'd they invite him?" I asked Willemien, both confused and relieved, since I considered Father Driessen an ally.

"I haven't the faintest."

In early January I had spoken with Father Driessen to let him know I wanted to marry Willemien, but that we still hadn't told her parents, because we were certain they wouldn't approve. Father Driessen congratulated me on the good news, and told me it would be best if I approached them to ask for Willemien's hand, because her parents were quite traditional and would appreciate the gesture.

But Willemien didn't like the idea. She said she wanted to do it her way and she told them about our engagement herself. Just as we had expected, their faces fell and the ensuing silence made it clear that they wouldn't support our plans.

So we had come to a stalemate; we were hoping Willemien's parents would change their minds, and they were hoping we would change ours. During that time, which lasted for more than two months, I hadn't brought up the wedding with Father Driessen again.

It seemed that the time to bring it up again had arrived, and that I'd have to do it in front of everyone. If this dinner had been arranged to get me to formally ask for Willemien's hand, it was fine with me. But something told me that was not why we were all there that afternoon.

Willemien sat down beside me.

"What if he's coming to marry us?" she joked.

"Great, let him marry us!"

After a while Willemien's father came into the living room. The armchair where he sat down was five meters away from us, a distance in keeping with the tepidness of our relations.

"Father Driessen is also dining with us tonight. He'll be here soon," my future father-in-law said slowly in Dutch. I understood him perfectly and replied, pronouncing my words carefully, "He's a good man. I'm happy to see him again."

He looked at me as if he understood only half of what I had said, then he turned to Willemien and began speaking so quickly that I couldn't understand a single word, as he often did to make me uncomfortable. I could tell from Willemien's face that it wasn't an important conversation, and I relaxed.

When the doorbell rang Willemien's father got out of his armchair and left the room without a word. I heard the front door open and got up to greet Father Driessen. Willemien's parents looked at me suspiciously when he greeted me effusively, in Spanish.

Dinner was uneventful. We had trivial conversations that I can hardly remember. But at the end of dinner, much to my surprise, Willemien's father asked the priest to what they owed the pleasure of his visit. That was when I realized that it was Father Driessen, and not my future in-laws, who had gathered us together.

Father Driessen replied that he had some good news about marriages between Dutch women and foreigners. He spoke in Dutch but translated what he said into Spanish afterwards. He said that the government was working on a new law that would allow Willemien to retain her Dutch citizenship in the event of our marriage. She would receive Spanish citizenship through me, but she wouldn't lose her own; she'd be a dual citizen.

Willemien looked at me with a victorious smile. Her parents looked at each other, defeated. The argument they had been making so relentlessly over the past few months had just evaporated, and they realized they had lost, right there in front of Father Driessen; they couldn't invent a new excuse for disapproving of our marriage. They had no choice but to give us their blessing right then and there, in front of the priest who would marry us.

That night, at my future in-laws' house, we set the wedding date. We'd get married on June 21 at the town hall, in accordance with Dutch law, and four days later we'd go to the church in Someren, where Father Driessen would preside at the bilingual, Catholic ceremony.

Willemien's mother, at least, was happy that her daughter was marrying a Catholic. Her biggest fear, at least until Someren had been invaded by Spanish guest-workers, had always been that her daughter would marry a Protestant.

I waited until after Pedro and Mariana's wedding to send a letter to my parents announcing our wedding. My mother replied that in the summer we'd have a party celebrating both unions. But the party never took place.

Her

On a break at work, I started with the forty-seventh person on my list. I typed the name into my computer when all my colleagues were out of the office.

I knew it wouldn't take long, that in all likelihood I wouldn't find him, but I thought I should try all the same. Sven Kils wasn't registered with the Dutch tax authorities. But I did find a Sven Kils in Germany through Google. I planned a trip to Berlin. I already knew that he was too young to be the one I was looking for, but that didn't stop me from tracking him down. I was almost halfway through my list, and after investigating forty-six names, calling and visiting over eighty people, I couldn't imagine discarding one of these names without at least speaking to them. I had to be systematic, organized.

Friday I took the day off and flew to Berlin. My flight left at 6:50; it was half-full and I was alone in row seventeen. I arrived in Berlin early in the morning. I had done an internet search for directions from the airport to Sven Kils's office, and had the printout with me. After landing it took over an hour to get to the office. I hadn't called to make an appointment with him. Sometimes I did, sometimes

I didn't. This time I thought that if he wasn't in, I'd ask his secretary or one of his colleagues. Sometimes it was more helpful to do this than to speak with the person directly.

The city was bustling. It was different from Amsterdam, where it was difficult to tell if people were going to work, school, or coming home from a night out. In Berlin it was clear everyone was going to work. Or perhaps it was just that the U-Bahn had deposited me in a business district.

I arrived at reception in a tall building and told the receptionist I was looking for Sven Kils. Without uttering a word, the girl motioned to the elevators. At first I thought she was being rude, but then I realized she was on a phone call on her headset. I walked over to the elevators, wondering how many floors there might be. Hanging next to one elevator was a directory of all the offices in the building. The Sven Kils's design studio was on the tenth floor. I was the only person who got in the elevator.

When the doors opened I found myself in another world. The cold marble and high ceilings of the lobby had turned into a world without walls, bursting with warm colors and playful objects. I didn't feel any more or less welcome than I had in the lobby, but I was struck by the contrast. Color was splashed across every surface: desks, columns, chairs, and carpets, but also giant balls of yarn and huge dice. The whole floor was so over-stimulating that you could hardly see past where you were standing. I was facing an empty desk. I walked over to it and, with the change in perspective, saw two guys who had been hidden behind a column. One of them approached me.

It was Sven Kils. He was twenty-five years old and spoke in a fast Berlin accent that was difficult for me to understand. I asked if he could speak more slowly and he looked at me like I was stupid. But I didn't mind.

"I like your office," I said, just to show him I knew German.

"This is our second year here, it's a little worn now, but for visitors the novelty doesn't wear off."

"How many people work here?"

I wasn't remotely interested in his business, and I have no idea what he said. I just wanted to make sure he wasn't the one I was looking for.

"Have you ever been to Holland?" I asked, getting straight to the point.

"Plenty. We have good clients in Amsterdam, I go three or four times a year."

His misuse of the word "plenty" made me laugh. He didn't think it was so funny. I was overcome by the need to get out of there. I had laid eyes on Sven Kils; he was too young, brusque and arrogant. But I had an important question for him.

"Was your father also called Sven Kils?"

He didn't answer. He looked at me surprised, uncomfortable. I suddenly felt sorry for him. In a flash I understood why he was the way he was, he had lost his father too young, which is why he'd had to make himself more important than he was. But perhaps I was mistaken.

"My father doesn't work here any longer," he said, his face tense. It wasn't clear from his response whether or not his father's name was Sven Kils.

"Did he ever live in Holland?"

"My father never crossed the German border in his whole life."

I thanked him and said I had to go. He was agreeable and I was grateful not to be questioned about the reason for my visit. I could have lied to him, but after his last response I didn't' think I would have been able to hide the truth.

I was wondering what else I could do with my time in Berlin when the elevator stopped on the fifth floor. A girl carrying a rolled-up poster got in. She was a little younger than me and wore a long black dress, one that would make a great party outfit with an eye-catching necklace, but with the modest scarf she wore it was perfect for the office. It occurred to me that I should take more time putting my outfits together; I was wearing some comfy jeans and a black turtleneck sweater.

The girl pressed the button for the twenty-third floor. I was going to say that we were going down, but the elevator started going up. The girl unrolled the poster and flattened it against the mirror. She asked me what I thought.

It was approximately fifty by sixty centimeters. Photos, postcards, and magazine clippings were pasted randomly against a white background. The first thing I noticed was that everything was yellow, or yellowish. There was a flower, a baby's blond hair, an apple and a banana, a yellow car with a caravan, the yellowish interior of an old home, a piece of a card with a quote about love written in pencil.

"It's a mood board, for inspiration," she said. "How does it make you feel?"

I was used to replying "m-hm" to strangers. Like when a woman started telling me her life story in line at the supermarket: had she closed the lock on her bike properly, or which sausages she liked best. Easy conversations: I'd answer "m-hm" and they were satisfied. But this was different, the woman in the elevator really wanted my opinion, she wouldn't be satisfied with a simple "m-hm" and a nod.

"Don't think about it too much, just say what comes immediately to mind." It hadn't occurred to her that I might not want to answer her question. She moved the poster left and right, up and down against the mirror. I saw how the light changed as she moved it. I pulled gently at the upper right-hand corner of the poster to place it next to the mirror, rather than on top of it. Her hands followed mine. Then I looked at the poster in its reflection.

An energetic "ping" announced our arrival at the twenty-third floor. She moved toward the door. I glanced at the poster once more and said, "It represents a moment of happiness, just before an accident happens."

The girl stood there frozen, staring at me. I wondered if she hadn't understood me, or if she thought I had captured the spirit perfectly.

"Can I ask you one more thing?" she said.

I got out of the elevator and followed her into an office. Her name was Jenny. It was her job to bring the characters and the settings of books and screenplays to life. She translated words into images so the director, actors, location scouts, and stylists could familiarize themselves with these characters and settings. It seemed to me her job was the exact opposite of a writer's. Whereas a writer translates mood and fantasy into words in black and white, Jenny did the opposite, translating those words back into original sentiment.

"What about the poster makes you think of happiness?" she asked.

"The combination of a caravan, a blond boy, and a love letter, all of those images make me think of a family.

"And what about the accident?"

"The accident's not there. It could happen at any moment; perhaps it's because these are all static images, frozen in time. Why freeze time unless it's to avoid an accident?"

She was taken aback by my explanation.

"I've never thought that way about a photo," she said, looking at the poster again. "That's why I like sharing my work with strangers, because the people who are going to see the film are strangers."

"It's just one opinion, my own point of view, it's colored by my personal experience."

Her face grew pensive. Then she looked at the poster again and said, "In the movie they won't be static images. Can you imagine what it would look like then? Can you look at the poster without seeing it as frozen in time?"

"In that case it makes me nostalgic for something that's been lost."

"Yes!" she said triumphantly. "That's exactly what I wanted to capture. I hope other people see it that way, too," she said enthusiastically. That's when I realized she was new on the job. "How did you put it before? Your perspective is a product of what you've experienced. Let's hope there are more people who've had the same experiences that you and I have."

I wanted to say that I certainly hoped not, that it was a cruel wish. But I knew that she couldn't possibly know what she was saying.

"What's the movie called?" I asked, though I didn't really want to know.

"I'm sorry, I can't tell you that. You might hear it in the hallways one day, when it's wrapped and they let us talk about it."

"I don't work here, I'm on my way back to Amsterdam."

"What are you doing here?"

"I was looking for someone, but I didn't find him."

"Who are you looking for?"

"Sorry, I don't really have time to go into it, I should leave."

She looked disappointed. I could have stayed and talked to her for hours, because it had just turned ten and my train didn't depart until 3:45. But I decided to leave her. She had upset me somehow, and I didn't want to open up to her.

On the way down, the elevator stopped on the tenth floor, but no one got in. For ten seconds I glanced around the office of a man who didn't want to talk about his father. I wondered whether he, too, might once have had a conversation with his boss about being friendlier in the office. Probably not, because he was his own boss, and perhaps because he was able to talk about his mother.

Out in the street, the air was clear and dry. My hair behaved differently in the soft breeze than it did in Holland. It moved more freely and returned to its original style more neatly after being blown around.

I had time to kill. The Prenzlauer Berg neighborhood seemed like a good place to go. I got off the U-Bahn at Schönhauser Allee. I walked past a shopping center, in search of a more peaceful place. The cold streets of the old laborers' district felt familiar to me. I wandered along wide streets lined with bars and wondered whether anyone would think I was German, whether I looked like I fit in. Prenzlauer Berg had been fixed up, but it retained the same feeling as it had years ago. I imagined Jenny lived on one of these streets.

I had an early lunch in a bar and continued walking in the direction of the train station. I walked for a good hour, and I felt the grandness of the city around me. My country was little.

I thought about the conversations I'd had that morning. I noticed a kind of leitmotiv of dismay. I realized how thin the line between a normal conversation and the memory of a disaster was. I had upset Sven Kils with an innocent question about his father and Jenny had upset me with a well-meaning, naïve comment about my past. I shouldn't hold it against Jenny, any more than Sven Kils should hold it against me. Fortunately. When you take a step back, life can seem extraordinarily sad.

It was already dark by the time I boarded the train. On the way home I thought that Karen Abrams would have liked to meet Jenny. Back in Amsterdam I learned I was right. It was midnight on the dot when I walked into her bar.

"In another lifetime I made mood boards," Karen Abrams said when I told her about Jenny's job. "See those photo montages on the walls? They're kind of like mood boards."

The walls of her bar were covered floor to ceiling with old photos of the neighborhood.

Him

In the summer of 1964 Willemien came with me to get to know my town, my country, and my family. My in-laws wanted to buy their daughter a very expensive plane ticket so she wouldn't have to make the long train trip, but she said no, as she did to all her parents' offers, and together we boarded the special train that Philips had chartered for its Spanish employees. When we arrived in Cáceres we boarded the bus for five neighboring towns in the Jerte Valley.

The bus stopped in the town square and Willemien and I disembarked along with four of my colleagues. My mother and sisters were waiting for us. They all greeted me first, then Willemien, looking her up and down several times, unsure of what to say. Until Willemien said in Spanish, "Pleased to meet you," with her winningest smile, and we set off for home.

Willemien had hardly crossed the threshold when she decided that our families were total opposites. She was confused by the warmth of their reception, and she asked me how I could have left such a loving family behind for her cold country. I remember being tempted to list all the disagreements that were obscured by the joy of such a happy reunion. But I didn't. I just told her I had to leave to earn more money. And since I kept my mouth shut that night, I kept it shut forever. I never told her about Mariana, and Willemien never asked.

Those first days of that visit I also saw my country through the eyes of a foreigner. I showed Willemien chestnuts, oaks, and ilexes, mountains and valleys, cherry trees and olive trees, the wild nature of the rivers, with their ravines and waterfalls.

But her favorite thing was something I had never really noticed. Something I had seen without really seeing and which she stopped to examine carefully. She called them the "stone fields." She could spend hours on end staring at these gigantic stones. Stones which her country, built on sand, did not have, and which here, in my country, she could touch and embrace.

One night that summer, during a family dinner, Willemien expressed her fascination with these large stones scattered through the vast fields. So Mariana told her that in Cuacos de Yuste there was a magnificent one right on the center of town, surrounded by houses.

The next day Willemien insisted that we go to Cuacos, so we went. We walked through the town, discovering its sites and its landscapes. I had never been before. Throughout the peaceful little town, Willemien would turn the corner before me and hide behind a column or in a doorway. When I found her, she asked me to kiss her quickly. She had yet to learn that many things she did without a second thought in Holland were frowned upon in my homeland. Deeply frowned upon.

The second time she asked me to kiss her I looked around and said no. She thought I was playing and tried again.

"Willemien, *lieverd*, not now. There are eyes watching us behind these curtains."

"That doesn't matter."

"It does matter. Here it matters very much."

It was probably the first time I had refused her a kiss ever since we had met. Perhaps that's why she reacted the way she did. Looking me straight in the eye she said Miguel would never have done that.

Bringing Miguel into it made me angrier than I would have expected. I answered her, glancing sidelong around us, trying to figure out if anyone could be eavesdropping on our conversation through an open window.

"Miguel never brought you to Spain. He's from a town in this same country, where the people and the customs are no different. He would have done exactly the same thing as me. All the men in this country do."

She remained silent and continued walking alongside me without looking at me. We were in my territory. Now it was her turn to deal with different customs, ones she didn't understand. Although I was angry that Willemien seemed not to want to learn the customs of my country, I fully understood her confusion. I also knew about her country's freedom. I, too, had grown accustomed to kissing in the street, and putting my arms around her without drawing attention. I whispered in her ear that I'd kiss her later, when I thought the coast was clear. She smiled at me, and that was the end of one of our first marital disputes.

After walking around in circles a few times, we found the huge stone Mariana had told us about. It was truly a magnificent stone, built into the walls of the houses around it, which were like woodland mushrooms that had sprung up on top of it. Willemien looked around in wonder.

"Here, long before there was a town, there was a vast field of stones," she said slowly, as if she were my tour guide. "There were stones of all sizes scattered everywhere," her voice had become lower, more thoughtful. She was writing a story in her head. "One day a man came to this stone field and he began to move them, to make room to build a house. While he was pushing one of these boulders he thought he'd be able to move it more easily if he split it in two. He tried, but it split into four or five different-sized pieces instead of two. He thought he could use the smallest pieces as bricks for building his house. And you know what happened then?" she asked, her eyes full of magic.

"No, tell me."

"His house was lovely and strong, and the other men from the region decided to build their homes near his. That's why the stones slowly began to disappear from the fields, turned into bricks of the homes they were building. But there was one stone, a very large one, which was indestructible. The story has it that all the men who built a house in that town each tried to break the stone at least three times. No one succeeded."

Two kids had wandered over and were listening to my Willemien as if she were a wise old grandmother.

"So the town continued to grow, and the story of the stone spread throughout the region. Some people even said the stone was cursed, or that it had a life of its own, and would get up and leave town of its own accord one day. But, day by day, the stone found itself surrounded by more and more houses and narrow streets. Such that in the end, even if it had grown legs to get up and go, there was no way for it to leave."

Willemien paused and looked at the two boys.

"What's your name?" she asked the boy who had come closest.

"Francisco."

"And yours?" she asked the other one.

"Francisco too."

"Okay. Do you want to hear the end of the story?"

"Yes."

"Some time later, two men from a neighboring town arrived. Their names were Francisco and Francisco, and they were good friends. Francsico told Francisco that they should use the stone to build the wall of a house. And Francisco replied that it was impossible to make bricks out of that stone. But Francisco said that they didn't need to make bricks, they could build their homes onto the stone. The stone itself would be a wall. So they'd only have to make bricks for the other three walls. Then others copied their idea, and that's how this lovely corner of Cuacos de Yuste came to be."

One of the boys asked, "Which Francisco am I?"

"Whichever you want to be," Willemien said.

"I want to be the one who built the house."

"Me too, me too," the other Francisco said.

"They both built a house, you can both be the Francisco that builds a house. You should each choose a house, that's all."

The boys hurried off to look at all of the houses around the stone, as if they had never laid eyes on them before.

Willemien and I returned along the same street we had taken earlier. In the distance we could hear the boys arguing over the same house.

That day, after our first argument, I fell in love with Willemien all over again. Mariana was becoming a distant memory of misunderstanding and pain. Willemien was my future.

Her

"How's it going with your list?" Karen Abrams asked one Tuesday night.

"Same as ever," I answered. "Sometimes I think *what's the point?* I usually get so caught up talking to the people I meet that I forget about what I'm looking for."

"Yes, I can imagine, the people you meet are so different," she turned away to make coffee for a customer. I paused for a moment before deciding to confide in her.

"I opened the box," I said, without elaborating.

She stopped making coffee and looked at me in astonishment.

"When?"

"Yesterday," I lied.

"What's inside?"

"Ash."

"What kind of ash?"

"I don't know."

"Cremains?"

"I don't think so. It looks more like paper ash."

I had never seen cremains before.

"I want to see it."

"I don't know, it seems quite personal."

"Personal? To you?"

She was hurt, but I couldn't help it. It really was a personal matter. Of course, it was someone else's business, but it was still personal, and I wasn't sure I wanted to make it into a circus. Plus I wasn't completely sure that it wasn't cremains. I didn't answer. She said something under her breath and added, "It's so typical of you!" Having raised her voice, she lowered it again to a near whisper.

"Let's not forget you stole it!"

I was used to telling her my stories. Karen Abrams always listened attentively from the other side of the bar. She believed everything I said, she found it interesting and always wanted to know more. Plus, she never forgot a thing and I liked the fact she knew what was going on. My stories were like a television series for her, or a movie. Something she watched but didn't play a part in. Until she asked if she could see the box. I hadn't expected her to want to become involved. I realized I didn't want to show it to her, but I sensed that our friendship, or our proprietor-customer relationship, or whatever it was we had, hung in the balance.

"Okay, I'll show you," I eventually said. "Just come to my place, alright?"

"I can't leave the bar right now. I'll come after closing?"

"Alright. I'll wait for you at home."

I left on my bike, realizing that it would be nice to arrive home knowing that my day wasn't completely over, that I wasn't alone for the night quite yet.

At twelve thirty Karen Abrams called to say she had just closed the bar and was on the way to my house on her bike. I put the kettle on and waited for her with the box on the dining room table.

She looked tired, but happy and excited to see the box.

She sat down opposite me at the table and touched its lid. She knew she ought not to open it until I had given her permission, but I was surprised by her impatience. Until then the box had been a secret between me and the dead man. Now there would be more than just us two, and everything would change.

"Can I see?" Karen Abrams asked.

"I'll open it for you."

I put my hand on the lid and opened it carefully. I had to do it slowly, painstakingly, because a quick movement could create an air current that would displace the ash from the box.

"Look," I whispered, as if it really were someone's cremains.

"Don't worry, I won't touch, I just want to take a closer look."

"Do you think they're cremains?" I whispered in her ear.

"Two weeks ago we cremated my mother," she said, impassively.

I was taken aback.

"Why didn't you tell me?"

"I don't like to talk about things that make me sad."

We looked at the ashes in the box together.

"It's too dark and too fine to be cremains . . ."

"Then what do you think it is?"

"It's burnt paper."

"Are you sure?"

"Have you moved it around a little?"

"No."

"Do you think we could?"

"I don't know."

"I think we should," she said decisively.

I still wasn't sure, but she was already looking around for something to stir the ash with.

"I'm thinking we need a letter opener or something like that, I'd rather not use a piece of cutlery, that doesn't seem right."

I also glanced around; I didn't have a letter opener.

"What about one of those sticks for stirring paint?"

Without hesitation I closed the lid of the box again and went to my studio.

"Don't you trust me?" she asked. I pretended not to have heard her. She didn't repeat her question.

When I returned to the living room I found her looking at the photos on the wall.

"Are these your parents?" She pointed to a photo from the eighties, my parents head-over-heels in love, holding a baby.

"Yes, that's my parents."

"And this tiny thing is you?"

"Yes, that was me."

She looked at me and glanced away. I went over to the box and opened the lid slowly. Then I gave her the wooden stick.

"You want me to do it?" she asked anxiously.

"Yes."

She stabbed the stick into the ash and moved a heap to one side.

"No doubt about it, this is paper ash," she said.

"Are you positive?"

"Yes."

She moved another heap aside and then we saw it: there was something else beneath the ash.

Karen Abrams sat down and invited me to sit beside her. She had taken over, she had made herself at home, and I thought it was good. I took the chair from the opposite side of the table and moved next to her. She scooted her chair closer to mine.

"This way we'll both see it at the same time," she said as she inched the box to the edge of the table. It made me think of two kids secretly dissecting a lizard for the first time, and how afterwards they swear never to do it again.

Karen Abrams looked at me and put the wooden stick into the box. She carefully made a crater in the ash so we could see what was underneath it.

"See it?"

I nodded. She blew gently on the crater she had created. An iron ring appeared beneath the ash.

"There's a secret compartment under there," she said excitedly.

I knew Karen Abrams wanted to lift the ring. I knew she wouldn't be satisfied until there was nothing left to discover, but I hadn't thought she'd be so quick to act. She put the wooden stick down on the table, rubbed her fingers together, winked at me, and put her hand into the box. Her first, gentle attempt to pull the ring didn't do a thing, so she pushed her chair back, gathering her strength, placed her left hand on the edge of the box, and give the ring a yank with her right.

It made a soft, hardly audible sound, a slight click made by the separation of two parts, which had been together for a long time: the sound of something opening.

Then I saw black ash flying around my dining room. It started above the box and spread around the room. Little black spots that floated to the ceiling and descended, dark little particles that flew toward the windows and into the glass, falling on the edges of the window frames. Ash that stuck to the walls, and came to rest on the sofa. In silence.

Karen Abrams opened her hands in front of her like a tray. Flakes of ash fell on her palms and her fingers. She had a steel ring around her right index finger, attached to a small panel of wood.

We looked around in silence. A constellation of black holes appeared on my pale wooden table, surrounding the box. I didn't dare look into the box until the dance of the ashes had ended.

When the air had cleared, Karen Abrams brushed off her arms, and the ash on her hands fell to the ground, too. She carefully laid the wooden panel on the table and we both looked inside the box.

We were stunned into silence.

"Biztresa," Karen Abrams said, smiling.

"Bistraze?" I said.

What was hidden in the box was a word. A word we couldn't pronounce.

Him

When we returned from our first holiday together in Spain, Willemien's parents offered us a house they had bought in Someren. Willemien lost her temper and accused her parents of trying to keep her in town, and said that we'd find somewhere else to live.

I liked the idea of living in a house in Someren at first, and I was a little appalled by Willemien's rejection of such a generous gift.

"We don't need their help," she said emphatically.

"We don't need it? What do you mean? How are we going to buy a house? You don't want to live at your parents' while I'm living at the camp forever, do you?"

"We can find a house without their help, where we want to live: Eindhoven!"

"Why Eindhoven? I know *this* town, I know how to get around . . . *Lieverd*, I don't want to start all over again somewhere else."

"In Eindhoven you'd be closer to Philips, you'd save time on the commute."

She was right, but I had my own logic. I didn't want to be too far from my compatriots at the camp: they were my friends and they kept me grounded. In Someren I could walk by a bar and meet people I knew, just like at home. Eindhoven seemed like a real city, a big place where no one knows anyone, and the idea of feeling like a newcomer all over again made me anxious.

The next day I spoke to Father Driessen, to ask his advice about what to do, and he helped me much more than I had hoped. He told me Philips was building new camps in Eindhoven and Maarheeze.

"Maarheeze will open next month but Eindhoven will probably take until next year. The camps will have better facilities and as soon as they're done they'll relocate everyone. The camps in Someren will be taken over by other companies."

"Where is Maarheeze?" I asked, surprised. It had never occurred to me that the camp in Someren might cease to exist as I knew it.

"It's south of Eindhoven, about twelve kilometers from here."

"If everyone's in Maarheeze and I'm staying at my in-laws', how will I get to work? The Philips bus won't pass through Someren anymore, will it?"

"Don't worry, now that you're married the company will help you find a house in Eindhoven. Lots of Philips employees live in the De Strijp neighborhood, and when a family leaves, they offer the house to other employees. Recently they found a house for a guest-worker from Middelbeers who brought his wife from Spain. You need to speak to your contact in HR. He'll help you."

Just like when I decided to sign up to go to Holland, the day I decided to ask for a house in Eindhoven was preceded by a night full of strange dreams. This time I dreamt that we were going to live in a house with extraordinarily large windows. I arrived home after a long day of work and the door opened and closed behind me of its own accord. The house said good evening to me and the flowers in the garden turned to watch me arrive. There were books on the shelves that tried to push their spines out past the others, inviting me to take them. Everything was alive. Through one of the windows I saw my house's chimney going over to the neighbor's house for a chat. Although Willemien didn't appear in my dream, I knew the house was hers, that she had planted the flowers and chosen the books herself. When I awoke I knew that we'd end up in Eindhoven.

I spoke to the HR boss and soon they had allocated us a house. A few days before they moved the camp from Someren, Willemien and I moved to the workers' neighborhood, De Strijp. Employees of a cardboard factory from Helmond moved into the camp that had been my home.

Willemien's parents rented the house in Someren to a Dutch family, but only for a year, because they still hoped that Willemien would come to her senses and accept the gift. But we never returned to Someren.

We lived in De Strijp for more than ten years. That first year there were very few Spaniards in what was a predominantly Dutch community. They had moved from the rural northeast of Holland years ago to work for Philips, and gradually they moved to other parts of the city, to homes they bought, making room for new immigrants.

In the years that followed I ran into compatriots from the Someren camp, as well as others from different camps, whom I only knew from work. I'd see friends, who had always been single, walking down the street with their Spanish wives. The neighborhood filled up slowly, because in the beginning the Dutch government permitted only the wives to come, not the children. Later, I'd see the same friends with their Spanish wives, followed by three or four older children who had been waiting in Spain for their parents to get permission to reunify the family.

Once in a while, very seldom, I imagined I was one of them, and that Mariana had come to live with me, along with two totally Spanish babies. But the vision vanished, never to reappear, on the day Willemien told me she was pregnant with our first son.

Willemien knew from the very beginning that it was a boy and we'd name him Arjen, after her older brother, who'd died from an illness at the age of ten.

I understood her decision and I accepted it, despite the fact that I wasn't used to being told how things were going to be without having any say in the matter whatsoever. But she had a good reason, and the name was easy to pronounce, though it would be difficult for Spaniards to read. I sent my family a postcard with pictures of Eindhoven, and on the back I wrote the boy's name, though he was hardly the size of a chickpea in Willemien's belly: "His name will be Arjen, which is pronounced 'Á-rien.'" And I told them about Willemien's brother, to explain why their first grandson would not bear my name, which was my father's and my grandfather's, too.

Although I had thought I was doing the right thing as a father-to-be, proudly announcing my little one to my family, Willemien gave me a telling off when she learned I had told my family our son's name. In Holland you don't reveal a child's name until it is born. It was frowned upon to ask an expectant mother what she was going to name her child: it was bad luck to say the baby's name before it was born.

From that day I stopped thinking of my son by his name, because I was afraid I might let it slip.

And then one day in May 1966 I became the father of a blond, blue-eyed boy. He looked like an angel, and that's what all our Spanish neighbors in Eindhoven called him, because they still hadn't learned Dutch and couldn't remember my son's name.

Suddenly this tiny, bleating creature commandeered our time, our space, our thoughts, and our hearts. I no longer went to work in the factory to send money to my family in Spain, I went so it would be possible for this bleating creature who grabbed my finger with his soft, pink hands to eat, grow, speak, and walk.

A lot changed when our first son was born. Willemien's parents realized that their daughter would give them grandchildren who would babble away in both Spanish and Dutch.

Arjen grew up in a street along with boys from Extremadura and Andalucia, and attended school with pale, blond boys. Soon he was speaking perfect Dutch and Spanish.

After her maternity leave ended, Willemien had a hard time going back to work, and though she continued to design clothes, she reduced her hours to be with the boy and to study art history on her own. Some afternoons she'd go to the Van Abbe modern art museum with Arjen and return with her eyes sparkling, hiding ideas that it would take me some time to discover.

A few months later she began painting pictures in the attic, and when the weather permitted, in the garden. She bought an artist's easel, paints, paintbrushes, and lots of canvases, and she began wearing a painter's smock, which became more colorful by the day. Sometimes I'd come home from work and she was coming down from the attic with a smile on her lovely, red lips, which meant that she'd finished a painting.

In the garden she painted flowers and windows and houses and Dutch skies, whatever she could see from where her easel stood. But when it was too dark, or when it rained, as it frequently did, she worked in the attic, painting Extremaduran landscapes. She painted what she remembered of my homeland, or she reinvented it.

One day she showed me *The Stone-Houses*. It was her story about Cuacos de Yuste, told in five paintings.

I liked them because she had painted them, and because they made her happy. But it was hard for me to understand how she could spend so many hours in front of a canvas, applying stroke after stroke. Nevertheless, I was delighted with my new Willemien, who received me at the end of each workday as if I were her hero.

The first few years of our eldest son's life also brought about a big change in Willemien's relationship with her parents. She frequently traveled to Someren so her parents could see Arjen, and sometimes she even left him with them for the weekend.

They still had misunderstandings and arguments, but Willemien seemed to have forgiven them for all the obstacles they had placed between her and her dreams, and given them a fresh start. In response, her parents made an effort to appear less displeased by my presence in their family and by the artistic ambitions of their daughter.

When Willemien told her father she had been painting for a long time, the first thing he said was that it was nice she had a hobby, since she didn't have to spend so much time looking after Arjen anymore. His emphasis on the word *hobby* was so obvious that the conversation ended there, without Willemien offering her father so much as a glance at some of her recent paintings. She would have loved to show him what she had been able to do with a paintbrush, because her parents loved art and had always encouraged the development of her appreciation for art. But for them making art was a world apart from looking at it. Willemien's parents believed that artists led strange, erratic lives and didn't want to see their daughter become a bohemian who neglected her children and stopped visiting her parents.

Until one day Willemien's father surprised us with an unexpected visit. Well, he only surprised me. He showed up at the front door with his coat over his arm.

"I'm here to see my daughter's paintings," he said without even greeting me. I stood there, frozen to the spot. There was a small chance that Willemien might have invited him, but she had just left to pick up Arjen from the neighbor's house and sometimes she stayed for a chat.

"Willemien's not here," I told my father-in-law, hoping he would prefer to return when she was in.

"That's fine. I only need to see the paintings."

I still hesitated.

"It won't take a moment, and then I'll leave. So as not to bother you," he insisted.

"Don't worry, you won't bother me, sir, it's just that I think Willemien would like to show you the paintings herself."

"Of course, but she's not here, so you'll have to show me."

So I didn't have much choice. We went straight to the attic. I hoped Willemien wouldn't come home and find us poking around in her stuff.

In the attic, my father-in-law looked around at ten or twelve paintings, which lay scattered on the floor and against the walls. Fortunately he didn't touch anything, he just looked around quickly and said he'd seen enough.

When I shut the door behind him it dawned on me he hadn't said anything about them. I had no idea whether he was proud of his daughter's creations, or if he'd been disappointed. And since I knew that was what Willemien would ask me if she knew that her father had seen her work, I decided not to tell her about his visit.

A few days later Willemien's mother called to invite us to dinner. They wanted to introduce us to some friends of my father-in-law. It seemed important to them, so we accepted despite the fact we didn't really want to go.

Later, we'd regret not taking that meeting my in-laws arranged more seriously, because it changed Willemien's life. Her father's friends were a high-society couple who were planning to open an art gallery in Eindhoven and wanted to see Willemien's work.

Fortunately no one mentioned the fact that my father-in-law had seen the paintings. The future gallerists would come over and visit our attic, accompanied by my in-laws.

Her

When I walked through the door I could tell right away it wasn't a normal Wednesday morning. It reminded me of a crowded airport and I got that feeling I always get in my stomach right before takeoff.

When I got to my floor it all became clear. People were talking in small groups. I quickly joined one, the word "socializing" in my head, aware that my boss would see me "socializing." But the word was quickly replaced by "debacle."

It was one of the worst days the organization had had in years. It had come to light that they had lost 730,000 electronic tax returns. Apparently management had known for several days, but they had just gone public this morning. Despite the fact that "our people" were still trying to find the 730,000 returns—because some people still honestly thought they could find them—the news had leaked.

Now it didn't matter whether we found them or not. The damage was done.

I wanted to research Lianne Pérez-Horst, but nobody touched their computers that day. We went from meeting to meeting, preparing to face the press and for the public's reaction.

After work I hesitated before deciding to stop by Karen Abrams's bar. I wasn't sure I was in the mood to talk to her. It was possible she hadn't read the newspaper, but it was highly unlikely that at least some of her regulars wouldn't have heard the news.

I headed toward the street the bar was on and rode past on my bike. It wasn't very full. If there wasn't another customer who would butt into our conversation, I could deal with Karen Abrams. I thought about myself alone, at home, the phone ringing off the hook with calls from distant friends and acquaintances who'd be wanting to know what to do now that their tax return had been lost.

I opted for Karen Abrams.

I walked into the bar, like always, and sat on my stool. I waited for Karen Abrams to finish her conversation with a customer and come over.

"How's it going, cutie?" she asked, as always.

"Great."

"Any news? I didn't see you yesterday. I thought maybe you'd gone off to search for someone."

She seemed not to have heard the news.

"I worked late yesterday, went to the supermarket, and by that time it was too late."

"Have you learned anything about the word in the box?"

"No. I don't think it means anything. When I Google it there are no results."

"Really! I don't think I've ever gotten *no* results in Google." She looked thoughtful. "In other words, we have a box with a word inside that doesn't mean anything in any language in the world. Where do we go from here?"

"I don't know. I have to figure that out."

"Why don't you bring the box in some evening and we can have another look?"

"No. Sorry. I don't want to bring it out of the house. I'll think of some other way to continue our investigation." She looked at me mistrustfully and glanced away. After taking a deep breath she got a Coca-Cola from the fridge and filled her glass slowly.

"Want one?"

"Yes, please" I said as sweetly as I could.

"Who's next on your list?" she asked sincerely as she poured my Coca-Cola.

"Lianne Pérez-Horst."

"Aha, a Dutch woman who married a Portuguese guy." Her tone of voice was enthusiastic, as if she wasn't angry anymore.

"Isn't Pérez a Spanish name?"

"Could be." She glanced around the bar. "You want to stay for dinner? I made a special dessert just for you."

"Just for me? Why just for me?"

"I thought you probably had a terrible day at work."

She knew.

"It's not the end of the world. But it kept me from researching Lianne Pérez-Horst."

"Bummer. You want to go upstairs and use my computer?"

I was surprised to hear myself say yes. I had my own computer at home, but she was trying so hard to be helpful that I didn't want to turn her down.

"If you keep an eye on the place for a second I'll go upstairs and turn it on. I'll be right back . . ."

I stayed on my stool and looked around. What did she mean 'keep an eye on the place'? I hoped none of her customers would ask me for something, because I wouldn't be able to help them. The only thing I knew how to do was draw a beer. Karen Abrams returned in five minutes.

"Go on upstairs and do your thing."

"Thanks." I climbed the stairs to her flat, surprised by her generosity. I sat down on an old office chair and typed name number seventy-two from my list.

It turned out Lianne Pérez-Horst was a freelance journalist with her own blog. She lived in Eindhoven and was married to the son of a Spanish immigrant. I thought of the dead, nameless man. He was also a Spanish immigrant. Maybe Lianne Pérez-Horst's father-in-law knew the man who had died on the plane.

I took a look at her blog; there was a lot to read. That night, while Karen Abrams was serving her customers, I spent three hours in front of the computer reading all of Lianne Pérez-Horst's blog entries. Her words and the comments by her readers gave a clear description of her life, making it easy for me to view it from afar. I wondered whether someone who revealed so much about herself might also write about someone else. I wondered whether I might find myself described in her words, if she had written about that day in 1987 in Someren. But her story didn't date back that far. She had only been blogging about her life for the past four years.

I could approach Lianne Pérez-Horst in several different ways. I could send her a message with a few simple questions, I could call her, or I could just show up at her house, because all her contact information was online. It had been a long time since I'd been to Eindhoven, and it struck me as a good place to visit the following weekend. I nearly asked Karen Abrams if she'd join me, but as soon as I had the thought I realized it was crazy. Karen Abrams owned a bar, and our conversations were best held in a bar. I wouldn't know what to say to her on the train.

Lianne Pérez-Horst had two children. Saturday morning the family would get up early to go see her older son's soccer game. The bicycle race they had wanted to do afterwards had been cancelled by the sponsor on account of bad weather. Despite that, they had considered going on a bike ride, just the four of them. They liked adventure and weren't afraid of a downpour or the high winds that were forecast. But in the end they had decided to stay home and make an apple pie, leaving the bikes for another day.

The eldest son had asked for "a mud day" and his parents had promised that the next time they went out on their bikes it would be a mud bath.

It was all there, for anyone to read. Lianne Pérez-Horst's family life was open to the public. Looking at her life from the outside, it seemed utterly idyllic, unattainable, suffocating.

That Saturday afternoon when she was making apple pie seemed to me like the perfect time to ring her doorbell.

On the way home I decided to call Anneke, I was in a good enough mood to talk to her.

"Hello?"

"Hi, it's me." I was always "me" when I called Anneke and Jan. They didn't have another "me" to confuse me with.

"How are you, sweetie?"

"Good. Last week I was in Berlin, there and back in the same day, visiting my friend Jenny. She makes mood boards."

"Mood boards? What are they?"

I told her all about Jenny's life as if she were a real friend. While I was talking I thought about a study I had recently read, that said people tell sixty lies a day. I wondered how many lies I was telling as I talked at length about someone as if she really were my friend, though she wasn't.

"It sounds like a lovely job," Anneke said eventually. "When will Jenny come and visit you? Would you like to invite her over for dinner with us?"

"I don't know, Anneke, she's working pretty hard right now, but if she comes to visit I promise we'll come and see you," and that wasn't a lie. I liked to visit Anneke and Jan with someone else, to divert their attention.

"And when are you coming to visit?"

"I don't know, Anneke, there's some trouble at work, I guess you've heard about the missing tax returns, right? How about I come over next week?"

"Perfect, Jan will be happy to hear it."

"Good night."

"Good night, sweetie."

Him

The first painting Willemien sold at her parents' friends' new gallery was an Extremaduran landscape called *Airplanes in the Sky.* But in the broad, blue sky she had painted there wasn't a single plane, not even a cloud. Nevertheless, the swath of blue was hypnotizing, and people would stand in front of it for minutes on end, looking for a plane that wasn't there.

More than a year had passed since our first meeting with the gallerists, and since then Willemien had spent many hours on her paintings, and she had also given birth to our second son, Simon. We could have done things differently, the show could have been rescheduled, but back then we thought we could do anything. We knew that life could get even more difficult, and Willemien didn't want to lose the opportunity. Having a child at the same time as preparing for the show seemed to her to be a unique opportunity for creativity: creating both inside and outside herself.

At times I've thought that later she had to pay the price for all the energy she expended back then. But Willemien wouldn't be Willemien if she had done things differently.

Simon was born quickly, as if he knew his mother didn't have any time to waste. He was an easy baby, who soon learned to sleep like a champ. Many times Willemien said she wasn't surprised by his silent collaboration, because she had spent the pregnancy explaining to Simon that shortly after he was born she would have a show of her work.

They were intense, exhausting, happy months. We channeled all our energy into preparing for the opening, knowing that the day afterwards would be a vacuum we'd fill with rest and peace.

The day before the opening, Willemien spent all morning with the gallerists, hanging her paintings in the gallery. I stopped by after work to see how it looked and to help out if they needed it. When I arrived they were hanging the placards with the names of the paintings, while Willemien was nursing Simon in one of the back rooms. I spoke with the owners for a little while and they left to run an errand. We waited for Simon to fall asleep and then Willemien gave me a tour of the gallery's three rooms. She showed me each painting, one by one. Some I had seen before, others I had never laid eyes on.

The first room was filled with Extremaduran landscapes, the second featured the paintings of the stone houses, but when we came to the third room I was speechless. In ten paintings, Willemien had painted my dreams: the enormous, shining light bulb, the factory's blinding skylights, the house with the books that stood out from the shelves, begging to be read, the chimney of one house going over to talk to another.

"This is your room," she said with pride.

I was lost for words, looking at my dreams. I wondered how she had captured so well what had existed only in my head.

"How do you know the exact colors of my dreams?" I eventually asked.

"Because you told me about them so many times, I can see them, and this is what they look like in my imagination."

I took another look around the room. I imagined Willemien spending an entire day on one of these paintings, thinking about things I had made up, and meeting me afterwards with her painter's smile when I returned home from work.

"Why didn't you show me them before?"

"They look better here, hanging against the white walls, in good light. Do you like them?"

"Of course I do."

She stroked my cheek and left me alone with the paintings. I was struck by the similarities in the images. It was like Willemien had had the same dreams as me, like we had both made the journey to the light bulb factory together. I realized that in her inner world, there was plenty of room for me. I felt fortunate to share my life with a woman who came from a world so different from mine in so many ways.

A few minutes later, she was back at my side. She took my hand and led me back through the room with the stone houses. I stopped to look at one of the paintings more closely. In the window of one of the houses Willemien had painted there were two faces looking out at the street. I looked carefully and recognized Francisco and Francisco, the boys from Cuacos de Yuste.

"So in the end they built a house together?" I said joking.

"Yes. I like it better that way. If I had put them in two separate houses, they would seem lonely."

Willemien asked me what I thought of the show. I remembered I had already told her when we started our tour, and I realized she was nervous.

"It's going to be great," I said, with all the conviction I could muster, not being completely confident myself.

The next day, at the opening, I spent most of my time looking after Arjen, who had already turned three, and Simon, who was just seven months old.

In the years that followed, Willemien had four shows in different galleries and sold some paintings. But in 1971, when Robert was born, she put her brushes aside for a few months. Three children took up too much of her time. And then, there was no more room on our walls for more paintings, and Willemien didn't have a show coming up, so she decided to stop painting until she had time to prepare for a new show. The paintbrushes laid there for weeks, waiting for Willemien, and weeks turned into months without us noticing. When Robert turned one, Willemien told me she didn't think she'd ever paint again.

"Never again is a long time," I said, surprised. "Just wait, after a few years, when Robert is in school, you'll go up to the attic one day and before you know it you'll be painting again."

"You don't understand. It has nothing to do with the children. It's just that I've painted everything I wanted to paint. I think I should start doing something else. These past few years blank canvases always inspired me to fill them with color, but that doesn't happen anymore. The blankness stymies me, the empty canvases don't speak to me. I don't know why." She looked at me, hoping I'd understand, perhaps even hoping that I'd be able to help her understand her creative block. But I couldn't hide that I was out of my depth. "You'll find another way," I said, "I don't know what it is yet, but one day I will."

In the years that followed Willemien bought art books and went to shows with the children, but she didn't make any of her own work again until life dealt her its first blow.

When Willemien fell ill we had been married for ten years. Her fatigue began after we returned from a holiday in Extremadura. After making the trip by train for several summers, we made our first trip by car in 1974. In the green Opel Kadett we had bought. At first we chalked it up to the long car trip and the change in climate, but a few weeks after our return she was still just as tired and her joints started to ache.

The doctors spent several fruitless months trying to discover the reason for her aches and pains. Eventually, the doctor who had called us in to give us the results of the latest tests told us that it would be best if we moved to a gentler climate.

"Give it a try for a few months, and in time you'll see how much better you'll feel in the Mediterranean weather. Even if you don't get better, you'll be able to carry on a normal life."

While images of the Andalucian coast, which we had visited that past summer, flitted through my mind, I looked at Willemien and realized she had fixated on his last few words: "Even if you don't get better, you'll be able to carry on a normal life."

Normal was a word Willemien hated. Normal is what her parents had spent their whole lives wanting her to be, what she had never been. When we got home after a silent car ride, Willemien was furious.

"He said I could live a normal life. What is a normal life? How can my life be normal if I'm sick, and whatever I have doesn't even have a name and can't be cured?"

"But *lieverd*, we've talked about moving to Spain many times. You'll see, you'll feel much better once we're there."

She looked at me, and I was surprised to see something new in those eyes I knew so well. I realized there was another Willemien inside her, a weak, helpless Willemien, who didn't have the strength to reply. It was the first time I really understood what was happening to her.

The worst thing about an undiagnosed illness is the uncertainty. Not knowing what to expect, not knowing whether the beginning of the end has arrived, or if it's just a rough patch. Faced with uncertainty, I was used to choosing a position—to considering the options and opting for the most appealing vision of the future. When I accepted that my wife was sick, I saw two options for surviving.

I could choose a version of our future in which Willemien faded away; I could begin to live life with the knowledge that she wouldn't be with me much longer. So that if she really was going to die in the next few months I would be ready to say goodbye. That way, if she eventually got better, it would be like an unexpected gift.

But I could also choose a version in which Willemien was too young to leave us, in which it was impossible to say goodbye because she wasn't going anywhere, to live from day to day knowing we were going through a rough patch, that everything would get better and return to normal. In that case, if fate dealt us a blow and took Willemien from us, it would be a brutal farewell, the loss would kill me, but I would have lived my last days with Willemien to the fullest, not with a Willemien I had already written off.

I had chosen this second version of our future when Willemien made me see there was a third way to cope with the uncertainty. She wanted to live each day as if it were her last, yet knowing that she wasn't going to die. Because knowing that she wasn't going to die gave her the strength she needed to conquer her illness.

This was our future. And we got to work building our new life by finding the pitch where we would play this final, decisive game.

The next day I called Pedro and asked him to find out where it would be easiest to get a job along the Mediterranean coast. I knew many people from Extremadura had left for Cataluña in recent years, so I wasn't worried about finding work. I was slowly getting used to the idea that, after twelve years, I would be returning to the warmth of southern Europe, if not exactly to my home.

Pedro called me a few days later and read me a list of ten or twelve factories near Barcelona where Extremadurans were working. I remember feeling depressed because none of the options Pedro gave me were very interesting.

That night, after putting the children to bed, Willemien and I had dinner and I told her what Pedro had said. But instead of asking me which factories they were, she acted like she hadn't heard what I'd said and asked me, "Do you know who Salvador Dalí is?"

"No," I said, thinking she was talking about some guy who could help me find a job.

"He's an amazing painter."

I was taken aback, trying to understand what this amazing painter had to do with anything, till she explained, "I heard that they just opened a wonderful museum. Do you know where Figueres is?"

"No."

"A few kilometers from the Mediterranean coast. North of Barcelona. It's a small town. I imagine it's similar to Someren. Let's move there."

She sounded as sure of herself as she had ten years earlier, when she said we should move to Eindhoven. But this time, instead of feeling worried, I felt relieved. It meant we wouldn't have to move somewhere larger than Eindhoven. It meant I wouldn't have to work in one of the factories Pedro told me about.

"But were will I work?" I asked, not expecting her to reply. But Willemien already had it figured out.

"We'll open an electronics store, selling and repairing televisions and radios. And when I'm better I'll teach painting classes, or English."

Her

It was around noon on Saturday when my train arrived in Eindhoven. At twelve thirty I knocked on the white door of a newly built house in a residential neighborhood. An eight-year-old girl opened the door, her father at her side.

"Who are you?"

I didn't know what to say.

"Can I help you?" the father asked.

One of the gusts of wind that had persuaded the happy family to forgo their bicycle ride roared past and somewhere inside the house a door slammed. I pulled the collar of my coat close and wondered how to start. I had imagined that the mother would answer the door, in which case I would have started with "I think you might be able to help me with something that's really important." Instead, I had been surprised by this beautiful girl who was looking at me with her big blue eyes, and I wondered if Lianne Pérez-Horst's husband might also be important.

"I'm looking for Lianne Pérez-Horst," I managed to say.

The man smiled.

"Darling!" he called into the house.

"Mama!" the little girl echoed.

"It's for you," the father said. Then he turned to me and added, "Come in, it's too cold to leave the door open."

As I walked down the hallway of their house, I was struck again by the familiar sensation of unwarranted generosity that I had felt with Karen Abrams a few days earlier. But it was unlike what I had experienced in Karen Abrams's flat. I knew these people, I had observed them, so in a way it was obvious they'd let me in, I already knew what they had wanted to do for the day, what they had ended up doing, and what still remained to be done. But I was also aware of the fact they knew nothing about me, and that it was therefore a leap of faith for them to let me in. For a moment I thought they might have recognized me, and that I had finally come to the right place.

I walked behind Lianne Pérez-Horst's husband, noticing the warmth inside the house. The dining area smelled like apple pie, and bits of dough, raisins, and apple skins were scattered around the open-plan kitchen. A cat jumped onto the counter looking for scraps and the girl scolded him.

"Friday! Get down!"

The cat looked at the girl defiantly and she pushed him off the counter.

"You know that's against the rules, Friday, sweetie. . . ."

Friday fell gracefully to the floor and crossed the room to a half-filled bowl of cat food next to the fireplace, his tail between his legs.

Lianne Pérez-Horst dried her hands on a rag and approached me. I introduced myself and could tell from her eyes that my name meant nothing to her.

"What can I do for you?" she said, gesturing to the long sofa. I sat down at one end and the eight-year-old girl sat down beside me. The older boy, the soccer player, must not be home I thought. The girl's presence intimidated me. The various scripts I had run through in preparation for this moment had vanished. The only thing I could do was tell the truth, just as I had done with Karen Abrams that very first time, but abbreviating it—not revealing too much.

"I'm looking for someone," the sound of my own voice soothed me, "and it might be you."

"Who are you looking for?"

"Someone who witnessed an incident in Someren a long time ago."

Lianne Pérez-Horst looked at her husband and they both smiled. My heart jumped. I had found them!

"Is it you? Was it you?"

My excitement was short lived.

Lianne Pérez-Horst said, "What are you referring to?"

If they were the ones, they would have known, and they wouldn't have had to ask the question. So Lianne Pérez-Horst wasn't the person I was looking for. But she did have memories of Someren, because her husband's father had lived there, in a camp for employees of a cardboard factory.

Lianne Pérez-Horst invited me to stay for lunch; they were having soup and sandwiches, and then we'd try the apple pie. We'd talk about Someren. Lianne Pérez-Horst's husband insisted I stay because the storm was at its peak and it was too dangerous to go outside. They had no intention of letting me leave until they had shared all their memories.

"There's always room at the table in our house, and food for unexpected visitors," he said. "It comes from my side of the family. I'm Spanish."

"He always says that," Lianne Pérez-Horst said. "But it's not only his family traditions that make us enjoy entertaining guests. My family has always been open and friendly, too."

Lianne Pérez-Horst put a pot on the stove and her husband went up to the attic to look for photos. I went to the kitchen.

"Why did you think we might be the people you're looking for? How did you find our address?"

"It's on the web."

"Of course, through the Chamber of Commerce. I've often wondered if I could get them to remove it, for privacy."

I could have continued the conversation along those lines, I could have said something about the Tax Authority, and then we would have talked about my job, and about her job, too. All very normal, appropriate, and a little standoffish. At that moment I could have decided not to tell her about the list. But I decided to go for it. I trusted her. I wanted to return the kindness of her hospitality. It didn't seem like a big deal: to talk about the list or not talk about it. But it turned out to be a critical decision.

I'll never know what might have happened if I hadn't told her about the list. And I don't know whether it would have been for better or for worse. There's no point thinking about it. It's impossible to go back in time and change things.

"Your name is on a list of names of people who might be the ones I'm looking for."

"My name? Or my husband's?"

"Your name. Lianne Pérez-Horst."

"Ah, so someone thought: Lianne Pérez-Horst's husband lived in Someren, she might know something."

I hesitated. Eventually I decided to say yes.

"Who is this person? Do I know them?"

"I don't think so."

"What's their name?"

"You don't know them."

She looked at me, slightly offended. The feeling of trust we'd had up until then vanished with that look. I decided to go further back, to let her know where the list came from and why I was looking for these people. So I told her everything. Halfway through our conversation Lianne Pérez-Horst's husband returned to the living room with the photos of Someren, but Lianne Pérez-Horst was no longer interested in their own memories, she was fascinated by my search and she told her husband exactly what I had just revealed to her. I realized how carefully she had been listening to me. Then I let her see the list. The soup, which was still on the stove, got too thick because Lianne Pérez-Horst spent a long time reading the list, looking for names she recognized. But not one of those hundred names rang a bell.

We were halfway through lunch when she said, "I want to help you."

She could have meant a thousand different things, but she had one idea in mind. She wanted to publish the list in the paper where she worked. She wanted to interview me and share my story with the world. She was absolutely sure her plan would work. There was no better option.

"There are people who have nothing better to do, and they'll begin searching on your behalf. Some people like this kind of mystery."

I was stunned. I had never expected such an offer, and I wondered if I had been naïve. I should have realized that a journalist would come up with something like this. I realized how her proposal would wrest control from me. It was both worrisome and comforting at the same time. I had been offered help before, by Karen Abrams and Ana Mei Balau, but it had never made much difference, because they didn't know how to help.

Right then Lianne Pérez-Horst seemed like the best person for the job. I agreed.

Him

Willemien travelled to Barcelona by plane, with Simon and Robert, while I took the car, Arjen at my side, the trunk stuffed to the gills and a large bundle on the roof rack. It was 1977.

When Arjen and I arrived in Figueres we were met by one of Mariana's cousins who was a sales rep for ceramic figures in the area around Girona. He met us in the flat we were renting that first year.

After emptying the car in front of our new home I left Arjen and Mariana's cousin resting in the flat while I drove to Barcelona to pick up Willemien and the boys at the airport. She was tired but in high spirits, and she suggested that we take a look around Barcelona before driving to Figueres. I had no desire to, because I was exhausted, but I wanted to give her what she needed to begin this new life far from her home. We entered the city by Gran Via. Willemien gazed out the window as if she were dreaming, and from time to time she murmured, "We're going to live here. The boys will grow up here, this is our home from now on."

We hadn't been driving through the streets of Barcelona for more than ten minutes when Willemien put her hand on my shoulder and whispered that she had changed her mind. She wanted to get to Figueres quickly to see Arjen. We left the city and got on the highway. The cars were full of people who knew where they were going; in my car two little boys and one exceptional woman, who had never seen the landscapes we were passing, slept.

I imagined that we didn't have a destination, that Arjen was with us and that the five of us were on an endless road trip, that we'd go as far as we needed to get to the place where Willemien would be what she had been once again. I drove in silence, knowing she was dreaming the exact same thing as me. We had talked about it before; she had often said that this trip was just one step in the process of getting well again, which we'd begun when we'd decided to leave Holland, before we even knew where we'd be going. We had a year of discoveries and hard work ahead of us, of adapting and getting settled, but we knew the results would be well worth it.

After passing Girona, the low winter sun shining brilliantly in an incredibly blue sky, Willemien said, "We're going to win," and I believed her.

After a few days of moving in and getting to know the area, of taking the boys to school and walking the streets of Figueres, I came to the conclusion that I had neither the energy nor the resources to open an electronic appliance shop. There were already several in town and it seemed like a huge risk in a small community, where everyone had known each other all their lives. But Willemien had been very clear that we'd open a shop in Figueres and I could tell by the way she talked that she still hadn't abandoned the dream. It wasn't easy to convince her, but in the end I won.

The case was closed the day that I came home with the news that I had found a job at the electronic appliance shop in the Plaza del Comercio.

"It's settled: I have a job," I told Willemien happily.

"A job? Or a shop?" she said, determined as ever.

"A job in a shop owned by very nice people. A place that already has customers and a reputation, plus it's well-located, in the market square. It's a place to start."

"What will you do?"

"I'll repair radios and televisions, but I'll also wait on customers if it's busy or if the other employee doesn't show up for work."

"I'm so happy for you, darling," she eventually said.

"Me too, *lieverd*," I said, kissing her on the forehead.

What I didn't tell her was that I'd had to convince my boss that I'd learn Catalan in a few weeks, because it was good for business. I promised him I would, and although he didn't seem to believe me at first, I convinced him with a few words of Dutch, followed by a phrase I pronounced with near-religious conviction: "If I've learned that, learning Catalan will be a cinch." He thought it over a few seconds, and extended his right hand to shake on it.

I hadn't told him anything about Willemien's situation, or about the fact I had three kids to feed at home.

I learned Catalan by listening and guesswork. Arjen, Simon, and Robert were learning it at school, and Willemien learned by listening to the rest of us stumbling along. I soon realized that though I might not speak it well, the customers appreciated the effort. After a few months, when they had seen me in the street with my three Dutch boys a few times, they forgave me my linguistic inabilities. Arjen was learning Catalan, and he spoke Spanish perfectly, but he still talked to his brothers, and sometimes even me, in perfect Dutch that impressed the Figuerans.

Bit by bit we settled into a routine that gave us peace and hope. It was a difficult year, in which I became the anchor of the family instead of Willemien. Arjen was eleven years old and was determined to survive the temporary absence of his strong, nurturing mother. Without even saying a word about it, he began to take responsibility for getting his brothers to and from school, for settling quarrels between Simon and Robert, or dashing out to the shops if we needed something for dinner.

At the time I didn't realize how much effort my son was making to ease my burden. Later, in hindsight, I was able to see how vital his help had been. A few years ago I talked to Arjen about it. And he said to me, "Of course you would have managed without me, Dad. We're built to survive. We adapt to situations, bit by bit, but we eventually adapt. Sometimes we think we can't take it anymore, but we get up the next day and it turns out we can. Especially when we knew there was a point to it all, that mother would get better, that normal life was just around the corner. And you're the expert in adapting, Dad. You managed in Holland, and if you were happy in a country that's so different and so far from your own, you'd find a way to be happy in Figueres, illness or no illness, with or without a responsible son. And you were."

"I'm just thanking you, son."

Arjen paused for a moment and said, "Don't thank me for being who I am. You brought me up."

When Arjen turned eighteen he went back to Holland to study. That day, when my son flew out of Barcelona, I recalled the words my father had said to me in the main street of my hometown, and my departure on the bus, time and time again. Before he left I told Arjen that his room would always be his room, that if things didn't work out the way he hoped, he could always return without regrets.

I already knew he'd never come back home, but I needed to say those words to him, in case things got off to a rough start.

That first year, Arjen lived with his grandparents, until he found a room in a student apartment in Eindhoven. After that he lived in the city and went to Someren once in a while to visit his grandparents.

I remember the day Arjen called to tell me they were knocking down the camp in Someren to build an industrial complex of offices and warehouses. Whenever he visited his grandparents he'd ride his bike around Someren to see what had stayed the same and what had changed in town. He took photos of the new buildings and sent them to me.

One day Arjen sent us a photo of a field in Someren with a highway in the background, and a burnt out car rammed into an ancient tree. The image deeply affected me. You couldn't tell what kind of car it had been, but you could tell that after it had burned, the firemen had sawed it open to get the driver's charred body out.

Arjen had witnessed the accident. He was riding his bike through Someren with his girlfriend at the time. He'd wanted to show her the places where he had spent his childhood, his grandparents' house, the streets where he played with his brothers, and the place his father had spent his first months in Holland after arriving from Extremadura.

The camp was on the outskirts of Someren, practically in Someren-Eind, so they took the bike lane that ran parallel to the highway. When they were halfway between Someren and Someren-Eind, they were startled by the sound of tires squealing on the highway behind them. They stopped to see where the sound came from, and before they turned around they heard the impact of the car's body against a tree next to the highway. The car was a smoking wreck, about one hundred meters away from Arjen and his girlfriend.

My son dropped his bike and ran over. You could hear only the sound of his clothes as he ran, and the sound of his shoes hitting the ground. His girlfriend ran behind him, and on both sides of the highway—nothing. No cars, no bicycles, no one. Arjen turned to his girlfriend and told her to go back and get on her bicycle and ride to Someren-Eind to call an ambulance.

When Arjen got to the damaged vehicle, the engine was already on fire. He could see that the driver and the woman at his side were covered in blood, and completely trapped by the body of the vehicle. He tried with all his might to open the driver's door, unsuccessfully, so he went around to the other side. That door opened and Arjen could see that the woman's skirt was on fire. He was filled with panic, pity, and helplessness, he was frozen; but then he realized that in the backseat there was a girl lying between the seat and the floor of the car. It was a hatchback, so he tried to reach the girl through the broken right-hand window but he realized he could only reach her leg.

The front seats were already on fire by the time Arjen opened the hatchback and leaned into the car. Leaning against the rear seats he could reach one of the girl's legs and one of her arms, he pulled her and lifted her out, and ran from the car, which was engulfed in flames.

Arjen held the girl for several minutes, not knowing whether she was alive or dead. He brought his face close to her soft skin. She would be seven or eight years old, she was blonde and pale, like an angel, Arjen once said, and ever since when he talked about the experience it was of the day he saved an angel.

The ambulance arrived and Arjen couldn't let the girl go, the doctors had to pull her out of his arms while they asked him if he was alright and whether he had been in the car too. But Arjen couldn't answer. While one doctor checked his pupils and asked him over and over if he felt any pain, he saw the other doctor treating the girl as if she weren't dead. After putting her on the gurney and into the ambulance they helped him get in the ambulance, too. Just before they closed the rear doors of the vehicle he heard a fire truck in the distance, and when he glanced up to look for it he saw the figure of his girlfriend pedaling back as fast as she could.

In the hospital they asked for the girl's name and date of birth.

"I don't know her, I was just passing by," he said in a near-whisper. And he got up and walked out of the hospital.

Her

Anneke hadn't said the woman was a psychologist. We were just going to see someone. When we got there I realized that the woman was more interested in speaking to me than Anneke, but I was just a girl and back then it didn't occur to me that if she wanted to speak to me it was precisely because she was a psychologist and because Anneke had asked her to analyze me.

"I'm afraid of flying," the woman said.

"I'm not," I said.

"Do you know why I'm afraid?"

"No."

"Because I don't understand how the plane can stay in the air." She looked at me expectantly, but she hadn't asked me a question. "Do you know why planes can fly?"

"They fly because they have wings, like birds," I said confidently.

"So you're not afraid of flying?" she asked again.

"No."

"Not even a little bit?"

"No."

Anneke wanted to say something but the woman motioned for her to keep quiet.

"Well that's wonderful, isn't it, not to be afraid of anything. You're very brave."

"Yes."

"Do you know other people who are brave?"

"I don't know."

"You can't think of anyone else?"

"No."

"Is Jan brave?"

I thought this over. The truth was I hardly knew Jan.

"I don't know. I think so."

"And Anneke? Is Anneke brave?"

Anneke was not brave. She was difficult. That's what I thought at that moment and that's what I said.

"Why do you say Anneke is difficult?"

"She's different."

"Different from. . . ?"

"Just different."

I didn't want to talk about Anneke. Talking about her meant talking about my mother, it necessitated a comparison, one in which Anneke always paled. Anneke knew this, and I knew it all too well. I suppose the psychologist knew it too, and that it was what she was trying to get me to admit. But if I admitted it then we would end up talking about my mother, and that was something I didn't want at all. I had so little to say about her.

"Why don't you tell me what home is like?"

"Which home?" I asked sincerely.

"The home where you live now."

"Anneke and Jan's house?"

"Yes, Anneke's and Jan's and your house."

"It's big and white," I said confidently.

"And your room?"

"My room is also big and white."

"Your room is big and white?"

"It's the room I sleep in, but it's not my room. It's Anneke's and Jan's, because they used to keep an ironing board and books there, but now they've moved all those things to the storage room and they bought a bed for me. Now I sleep there.

I slept in the ironing room for years. Living in somebody else's house. Not my house. Life carried on. I lived in a dormitory and then I found a flat for myself. It was a place to live. It is a place to live. But since I was eight years old I haven't had a home.

Anneke kept insisting that I see the psychologist. I never saw her regularly, but over the years I saw her a number of times. She always tried to get me to talk about my parents and I did everything I possibly could not to.

In time I learned to tell her the same things over and over again. I was afraid that if I told her everything she was asking me about that somehow I'd be giving her power over my thoughts. I was afraid she would make my memories of my parents disappear, to make room for Anneke and Jan. I was too young. I was alone in the world and didn't trust anyone.

Sometimes she asked me to draw; a few times she let me draw whatever I wanted, other times she asked me to draw Anneke, Jan, and myself at home. It made me feel like a lab rat. I always drew the same thing: a room with an ironing board, and another room with a sofa. The room with the ironing board was empty. In the room with the sofa I drew two people: a man and a woman. Depending on how much time she gave me to draw, I'd keep going: the room with the sofa slowly filled with a television, a table and chairs, a window with a view of the garden's trees and flowers, photos on the walls . . .

When I finished she asked me to describe the drawing. I described only what was in the picture. I described my drawing in minute detail, but I didn't say anything about the people I had drawn. Sometimes she asked me where I was, because I hadn't drawn myself in the house. I always said the same thing.

"I'm not there. I'm here, with you, drawing."

The last time I went to see her I was sixteen. When I saw her that day, I knew it was the last time.

It had been a while since I'd drawn for her. In that final session she got me to talk mostly about school and what I wanted to study in the future. I knew that I was nearing freedom, that soon I'd turn eighteen and leave home. I thought that in my room in some dormitory I'd finally find my path, and that was what being free meant. I had grand plans, that I didn't actually pursue until years later, but at the time I truly thought I'd begin my search right away.

"Would you like to live in a dormitory?" the psychologist asked me on that final visit. That was the day I lost my battle with her.

"Of course."

"What are you looking forward to?"

"Freedom."

"You're not free now?"

"No."

"What will you do with your freedom?"

I thought a moment. I could tell her anything. I had no reason to tell the truth, I had already lied to her many times. But for once I didn't lie.

"Search."

"For what?"

"People."

"Which people?"

I looked outside. Hesitating. Through the window I saw her garden, the bare trees, and behind them, her neighbors' windows.

"They're not really people. I'm searching for angels."

She looked at me, taken aback, and I felt the power I had gained by saying those words. She asked me another question.

"When you find the angels, what will you tell them?"

I hadn't thought about that. I had imagined an encounter in which words were superfluous, everything was so obvious that a mere look would suffice. But maybe she was right, maybe I should consider what I would say to them.

"What will you achieve by finding them?"

I imagined standing in front of him, or her, and feeling what I had wanted to feel for so long.

"What I'll achieve is peace, reconciliation, closure. A farewell."

She looked at me triumphantly. She had gotten through to me. I knew she'd want to keep digging along those lines, but I didn't let her. She asked a few more questions which I didn't answer. The hour was almost up when she asked one last question.

"Who are the angels?"

And she waited. She glanced discreetly at her watch, but she didn't say anything else. We sat there in silence a few minutes. Until I decided to say good-bye.

"I'm moving to Amsterdam soon to study," I said. "So today will be my last visit."

She looked at me, worried. She said she'd give me a list of psychologists in Amsterdam, so I could continue my "process" there with another professional. I said that wouldn't be necessary and bid her farewell. I was on my way out the door when she said, "I'd like you to think about my last question. Who are the angels?"

I knew I would never see her again so I finally told her what she had been waiting to hear for so many years.

Him

We survived that first year in Figueres. The Dutch doctors had told Willemien to rest and be patient, and we dedicated all our efforts to that in the months after our arrival. They had predicted that in time she'd feel better and we clung to this hope.

Despite the fact I thought we had better find a doctor for Willemien in Figueres right away, she wanted to wait a while, to see how she felt after a few weeks. A few months passed, and she kept in touch with the Dutch doctor who had recommended we move south. She had a lot of faith in him, because he was a lifelong family friend, and Willemien said she didn't need second opinions, they would only be confusing.

In the end, she did improve, very slowly, over the course of that first year. There were days full of ups and downs, good days and bad days, sad days and happy days. But mostly there was hope.

On the bad days, when I came home from the shop for lunch and Willemien was resting in bed, I would sit by her side and listen to her for a while. Because though she had done almost nothing all morning, she had read or written things, and she had much more to tell me than I could tell her about broken televisions and nosy customers. Lunchtime was our time together, the peaceful part of our day, when we shared secrets, smiles, and tears without Arjen, Simon, or Robert interrupting us, because they ate lunch at school.

In our peaceful, silent house I made the meals that Willemien had planned. I learned to cook during those first years in Figueres. Willemien asked me to buy vegetables I couldn't find at the market, so I bought the ones that seemed most similar to me. Then she told me what to do with them. I botched things a few times, like the day when I mistook a fresh head of lettuce for chicory, though I didn't know exactly what we were going to make with it. But when Willemien told me to toss the scraps of lettuce into the pan where I had mashed the boiled potatoes, I knew that we'd be eating a crock-up that day.

Then we'd eat, usually at the kitchen table, but occasionally I'd bring her food on a four-legged tray I'd built, if she didn't have the energy to get out of bed. I ate in the armchair we had put next to the bedroom window, where she sometimes sat to watch the street when she'd had enough of lying in bed.

During meals, Willemien talked nonstop. About a wide variety of things. And I loved listening to her. Some days she talked about art, others she told me about a news article about Figueres that she had read in *La Vanguardia* or heard on the radio.

Those first months she talked about people she had gotten to "know" by reading them in the papers, since she hadn't been able to get to know anyone in our new neighborhood. She talked about Dalí and his wife Gala as if they were our neighbors upstairs, and she talked about certain politicians as if they were distant uncles. I realized she needed contact with the outside world, that we'd have to do something so she'd be able to meet people, but it took me a while to find a solution, and I got used to talking about the news as if I, too, were talking about my best friends.

Willemien would expound upon certain topics for days. She could spend a week talking about how Dalí had made one painting expressly for a soccer team that had fallen on hard times, or how the famous surrealist painter had undergone a prostate operation. And it's not that she was trying to expand upon these subjects, she was just telling me what had been printed in the paper: that Dalí was going to have an operation, that Dalí had had his operation, that Dalí was recovering, and that Dalí had recovered. And after a few weeks with Dalí, she'd begin to tell me about some Dutch artist. Like the time she told me about Wim T. Schippers. I remember that day lunch had turned out really well and we were both quite contented. She said, "A few years ago Wim T. Schippers emptied a bottle of lemonade into the North Sea."

I looked at her, surprised.

"It was a performance," she explained, without explaining anything. "I wasn't aware of it at the time. It was in the early seventies, but I've known about it for years now, ever since I stopped painting and began paying more attention to the world around me again."

I don't know what the point of knowing that a Dutch artist emptied a bottle of lemonade into the North Sea is, but it's a fact I know. I know he did it, and that Willemien enjoyed knowing that he did.

After three months in Figueres a letter from Mariana arrived. She had never written me a letter before. So when I received the letter postmarked in Plasencia the first thing I thought was that Antonia's handwriting had improved a lot since the last time she'd written to me.

It was a spring morning, one of those days when you can sense summer is on the way, though the pavement still held the chill of winter. I opened the envelope without a thought and removed the neatly folded sheet of paper, which was covered with writing on both sides. I realized it wasn't from Antonia when I began to unfold it: after all those years I still recognized Mariana's small, confident handwriting. My heart jumped and I folded the paper back up. I was certain that in the letter there would be words that would carry me back to the distant past. I was afraid, so I didn't read it.

For days I wondered what Mariana had written about. I recalled the exact moment when I lost her, her words, and the pain in my gut. My thoughts carried me even further away, to the day, a few months before that, when I had started to lose her, the day I lost Pedro forever.

I considered which pieces of our past I could tell Willemien about, and which I could not share. In the end I decided that my past with Mariana was just that, the past, and since it wasn't going to become part of the present it made no sense to worry Willemien about it.

One afternoon at home, when the boys were unusually quiet and Willemien was sleeping peacefully, I opened the letter, which I had kept hidden in a book for days, and read it three times through.

Mariana told me that things could have turned out differently. That life is full of decisions and forks in the road that determine our future. What she was really saying, twenty years too late, was that when she decided to stay with Pedro and not with me, things could easily have gone the other way. That some decisions are impossible; that she would have been happy with me, too. And that she was truly happy I had found in Willemien the woman of my life. That knowing I had been fine without her made her happier than anything else.

That's when I realized that, though for years I had lived with Mariana's ghost and wondered what my life might have been like if she had made a different choice, things had been even more difficult for her. I had no mistakes to regret, I just had to learn to accept her decision, and though it had been difficult, it was over once I had accepted it. But for her it was different: as the days and months and years passed, while she watched me from afar and wondered what she had lost, she knew that whatever she had lost, it was her own fault.

For the first time I realized that my bad luck of falling for women who were torn between two men relieved me of a huge burden: being the one who has to choose. Fortunately I never had to choose between Willemien and Mariana. Mariana chose Pedro, and Willemien chose me. And that's how I've been able to remain faithful to my wife, while Mariana retained a special place in my heart.

I finished hiding Mariana's letter just as Willemien called me from the bedroom. I felt dishonest.

There's no such thing as a life without secrets. Couples have secrets, families have secrets, cities have secrets, countries have secrets. And I have mine. But it's also true that sooner or later, secrets eventually come to light.

A few weeks later another letter from Mariana arrived. I read it the moment I found it in the mailbox, in the doorway of our house, while the neighbors passed by, wishing me a good morning. Mariana was surprised I hadn't answered her letter. It hadn't even occurred to me to. She spoke as though I had made a decision to remain silent, when the fact is that the possibility her letter could be the beginning of a dialogue hadn't even crossed my mind. For Mariana, it was the first in a series of confessions.

In the months that followed more letters arrived, filled with glimpses into my brother's life. Mariana used these letters as a way to reveal things she had never dared say to anyone, and for my part they brought me closer to my brother. I stopped seeing him as a rival. At some point I think I even began to develop a little sympathy for this man who would struggle all his life to keep such a beautiful woman at his side. A woman who clearly would continue to dream about his idealized older brother.

I never wrote back to Mariana.

Her

I went out into the street during lunch for some fresh air. The sky was clear and the pavement was wet. I ate my sandwich while I walked around the depressing business district. Groups of people, with and without sandwiches, were walking everywhere. It seemed like it was customary for people who were walking and eating to greet each other. Even a smile or a nod would do. I disregarded these shows of fellowship: these people weren't my colleagues, why did I need to be friendly to them? I walked along staring into space, like I was lost deep in thought, when the only thing I was thinking about was trying to find a street where there were no pedestrians.

My path through the wide streets was unpremeditated, at each corner I decided which way to turn. When a quarter of an hour had passed I turned around and traced my way back along the same streets to the office. The return trip was quicker, perhaps because I had finished my sandwich and I just focused on avoiding other pedestrians. I was two blocks from my office when I stopped at an intersection. When the light turned green I didn't cross the street. I stood there looking at the buildings surrounding me.

I didn't see him approach me. One second I was standing there alone, the next second he was beside me. In front of me. He had left his bicycle a few feet away.

"Do you speak English?"

I could tell he wasn't a native English speaker.

I said, "Yes, I do," but I wanted to ask where he was from.

"I just wanted to say that you are very nice." An arrow straight to my heart.

"Thank you."

Such pain and such joy at once.

"I think you are very nice," he repeated.

"Thank you."

I'm sure I smiled.

He turned toward his bicycle and pedaled away. I watched his back. His hair. His legs. All at once I wanted to cry and I wanted to shout after him not to leave. I wanted to go have a coffee with him and tell him all my secrets. I wanted to know who he was and what he was doing here, and why he had chosen me.

But I didn't move. I stayed at the intersection. Looking at the traffic light across the street. I waited for it to turn red again, then green, then red.

When I eventually crossed the street I looked in the direction he had gone and saw him in the distance. He had propped his bicycle against a building and was standing next to it, his hands in his pockets. Watching me. I started walking back to the office again.

It was already getting dark when I looked out the window by my desk at the sky and wondered why I hadn't waved to him, or walked over to him. His words had echoed in my head all afternoon. I was "very nice." I wasn't sure what he had meant. I typed the word "nice" into an online dictionary. Pleasant, agreeable, friendly, sympathetic, cute, charming, attractive, congenial, adorable, seductive, pleasing, fantastic, cheerful, fun, pretty, lovely, hot, good-looking, magnificent, affectionate, beautiful, gorgeous, elegant.

Was I all these things or just one? At least I knew I was "very" whatever it was.

After work I kept an eye out for my cyclist all the way to Karen Abrams's bar. When I turned into the street where the bar was my phone rang. Although I knew it wasn't him calling, I wished it were. It was Anneke. I didn't answer.

It was two in the morning when Karen Abrams locked the door of the bar and turned out the lights. We sat down at one of the tables where a candle still flickered. It wasn't the first time I had stayed on after closing time. It seemed extraordinary to me to have the whole place to ourselves.

Karen Abrams was at her best when the bar was empty. A few months earlier, when I had stayed late for the first time, she had said, "After closing I don't have to be the owner or the waitress anymore. When everyone has left, I'm just another client who can sit down at a table or on the other side of the bar. If you stay past closing time, you're also no longer what you were. You're no longer a customer and I'm not going to serve you. If you want something to drink, help yourself, okay?"

"Okay."

"But tomorrow, if you come again after work, you'll be a customer again, eh? Don't think that once you've gone behind the bar you've earned a privilege for life!"

That night she had just drawn two beers when we sat down at the table. Karen Abrams made her usual gesture for "ah, peace and quiet"—opening her hands on the table while breathing deeply. Then she took a sip of her beer and said sweetly, "Have you learned anything else about the word in the box?"

"I haven't done any more research."

"See, I said that you wouldn't have time for it. Why don't you give me the box and I'll do it."

I didn't want to talk about it. But she was dying to find out what the word meant and why it had been hidden in a box with a false bottom.

"You've got to do something. And if you're not going to do anything then you should return the box to the dead man's family. I've thought it over. You could call the airline and tell them you took the box by accident and that you want to find the dead man's family."

"Yeah, I could."

"But I already know you won't. You want to keep it a little longer, don't you?"

"Because I feel like the dead man wanted to tell me more than he was able to. Because I always fall asleep on planes, and I didn't finish my conversation with him. And when I woke up, he was dead."

"Do you think he knew he was going to die, and that he wanted to tell you something before it was too late?"

"If that's the case I failed him, because I didn't let him keep talking."

"I know my mother told me everything she wanted to say before she passed away. It gives me peace of mind. I think that's really important."

I wanted to end this conversation. I'd had enough.

"I have to tell you something," I said mysteriously. "Something that happened to me today."

I told her about my encounter with the foreign cyclist. I repeated his words in English and they sounded made-up as soon as I said them. Like a screenwriter had written some bad dialogue. But that wasn't true. I had been there, it had happened, and it was magical.

"Things are always happening to you," Karen Abrams said.

"What do you mean?"

"Something like that would never happen to me. I see a lot of stuff happening from behind the bar, but none of it involves me. You're out there, in life. You do things. I don't. I watch things."

When Karen Abrams put it that way, I could see the difference between her life and mine, too. But why did it seem like I also watched life instead of living it? I considered exploring the topic further with her, but I quickly changed my mind. It had been a good day.

"If I were you, I'd go to the same spot on Monday and wait for him," Karen Abrams said, curious.

"He probably won't show up."

"Of course he'll show up. It's the easiest way to see him again. It's like a secret code. Everyone knows that."

I was happy listening to Karen Abrams speaking about her world. I was happy to be in her bar instead of somewhere else, some other bar, with the cyclist who thought I was "very nice."

"You know what? I envy you. But I'm happy for you, too. This could be something special. You're on the brink of a great love story."

The next day I stayed in the office during lunch. I remembered Karen Abrams's words. I thought about the love story. The shortest one ever.

Him

One day I made a mistake. I didn't go home after work.

Maybe it wasn't a mistake, maybe I had to go away to be able to come back. We can be strong, but not invincible, and I was tired and lost.

I was angry because I was tired and I hadn't been able to be strong enough. Doubt had made me weak. There were times when I lost all hope, when I thought that we had moved to Figueres just to watch Willemien die more slowly than she would have if we had stayed in Eindhoven. There were moments when I escaped from the grief by imagining a life with Mariana, and I hated myself for not being able to imagine a future with Willemien.

One day, after a quiet lunch in the bedroom with Willemien, I picked up a letter from Mariana that had just arrived in the mailbox and left for work. I read the letter on the way to the shop and I spent that afternoon thinking about a different life. By the time I left after work I had started to believe in that other life.

I know there's no excuse, that I should have thought of Willemien and the children at home, worrying when they realized I wasn't coming home. But I didn't think of them, because I couldn't. All I could think about was disappearing.

I hated myself and I was ashamed of my thoughts, my desires, my weakness. Part of me believed that Willemien hated me, too, and that they'd all be better off without me.

The way the mind works is extremely complicated. That's the only explanation I can come up with.

I disappeared without a word but I never arrived at my destination. Because the truth was that I didn't really have one.

Later I learned that the boys never knew about the real reason for my disappearance or that Willemien had suffered, because she told them that a distant relative had taken ill suddenly and that I'd had to leave without being able to say good-bye.

I just wanted to get away.

I took the last train from Figueres to Barcelona. In the city I walked around the neighborhood near Sants station all night. I wasn't the only one waiting for dawn to make or continue a journey. The eastern and western façades of the station were crowded with travelers sitting, leaning against the windows, waiting, dozing, reading, chatting. I decided not to join the tableau. I decided that the reason I was waiting for a train had to be completely different from everyone else's.

There was a moment, at four in the morning, when I passed a phone booth and thought about calling home to let them know I was okay. I didn't though, because I thought I'd need all the change in my pocket to be able to get somewhere.

When the station came to life I bought a ticket for a train to Madrid and spent the time till its departure reading a copy of yesterday's paper that someone had tossed on a bench. I remember that feeling of living in the moment, of not wanting to think about the past and not being able to think about the future. The freedom of worrying only about the present moment. Reading a page of the paper as if that page of the paper and I were the only two things in the whole world. I had no more plans, no more responsibilities. I washed my hands of it all and for once in my life I was completely alone. At first I felt free. But that didn't last long.

As soon as I closed the paper desperation set in: the moment after finishing the last page was a void.

I realized that freedom doesn't exist. If I didn't have concrete plans, I'd have to create each minute of my life from nothingness. Without a sense of purpose, each moment became a decision. I could board the train or not. I could go all the way to Madrid or I could get off at some other station. I'd have to continue choosing a path each second of my life, and that was a massive burden. At some point I began to miss the security of the life I was fleeing, the sureness of knowing what each day held, as much as it might exhaust me.

I ended up boarding the train, with the newspaper I had found in the station. I read it again. Everything, even the classifieds, many times over. I had never read the paper so carefully.

In Madrid I found a hostel. In a rancid-smelling room with traces of damp on the walls I read the paper again, until I fell asleep.

On Sunday at five in the morning I awoke with a start, I couldn't breathe. I opened the window, stuck my head out, and breathed in the city air several times. When I lay down in bed again I realized it wasn't my bed, and that I didn't belong there, and I decided to go out into the street.

I walked around the city, crossing paths with young men who had been drinking. I thought of Arjen, Simon, and Robert. Sleeping in their child-size beds. Near the Puerta del Sol I paused outside a phone booth, hesitating. Eventually I entered the booth and dialed our number in Figueres.

"Where are you?" Willemien asked, breathless, when she picked up.

I didn't answer.

"Are you alright?" she asked a little more calmly.

"I'm in Madrid."

"What are you doing in Madrid?"

"I don't know."

The line was heavy with silence. I was waiting for Willemien to ask me when I was coming home, but she didn't.

"Are you alright?" she asked again. I still couldn't answer the question.

"I'll call you back in a minute," I said.

"Okay." I heard her voice breaking. I felt her slipping away. I realized I didn't want her to slip away yet.

"Are the boys alright?"

"Yes, we're all fine."

"Sorry for waking you up."

I wanted to say something sweet, something special we'd say to one another, something simple, like giving her a kiss or saying, "see you soon, *lieverd*" but it all sounded forced, untrue, at odds with my behavior.

"I love you," she said. "And I understand you. I'm tired, too."

"I'll call you back in a minute."

"Alright."

After a few seconds I hung up the receiver. I put my hand in my coat pocket and realized that the letter from

Mariana that I had read on the way back to work on Friday was still there. I went back to the hostel and sat on the bed. I read the letter again. I couldn't understand what about it had made me want to leave my life behind. I fell back to sleep.

On Sunday I walked around Madrid and felt very far away from all the places I had ever been able to call home. The hours passed slowly, and little by little my desire to return was coming back.

Late that afternoon I headed to the station. I watched other travelers while I waited for the night train to arrive. I slept like a baby the whole way. Monday morning I called my boss from the station in Sants and told him that I'd had to go to Barcelona for personal reasons and that I'd get to work around noon. He didn't make a fuss, though I could overhear how busy he was, and that they really did need me in the store. But instead of feeling weighted down I was at peace with the idea that there were people who needed me.

On the train to Figueres I read the paper again. Each time I reread an article I felt free, like I was back in Barcelona, on a bench in the station waiting for a train to begin a new life. I decided it wasn't necessary to run away. I'd find ways to escape while staying.

When I arrived in Figueres I went straight to work. My boss didn't ask me any questions, he just showed me the television I needed to fix and said that he hoped I'd have it ready by the end of the day. I got straight to work repairing it.

At lunchtime I walked home slowly. I opened the apartment door carefully and approached our bedroom as quietly as I could. I found Willemien dozing. There was an empty plate on the nightstand. I stood there, watching her;

she didn't look sad or worried. I realized that it had been too long since I had watched her sleeping, that I hadn't been seeing her as she used to be. That moment helped me tremendously. I was happy to be back home, where I belonged. I wanted to touch her.

I took a step toward her and that same moment she opened her eyes. Instead of speaking, she bit her lower lip. I sat down next to her and she embraced me. I had nothing to say. I was empty. I thought about the articles in Friday's paper.

We never talked about that weekend.

I kept that newspaper for several months. I took it out whenever I felt like running away.

We rebuilt our lives, and there never was any need to discuss what had happened. That weekend was just another one of my secrets. A secret shared, of overwhelming loneliness.

Her

We were flying home from holidays in Greece. I had never taken a flight with my real parents. I was twelve years old and I was flying for the first time, with my other parents, Anneke and Jan. Anneke was my mother's sister, but she wasn't anything like her. She hadn't had any of her own children because she was unable to, but Anneke and Jan wanted children and were in the process of adopting a one-year-old baby when I was orphaned. When they became my guardians they wondered whether or not they should still take the boy; in the end they turned the adoption down. Maybe, they thought, that time would come later, when I felt more at home with them. But "later" never came. It was a shame. I would have liked to have a cousin.

Anneke and Jan loved to travel. When I moved in with them they had recently returned from Italy, and they wanted to show me photos of their trip. Sometimes they traveled by car, when they went skiing for example. I didn't go with them. I never wanted to get in a car again. A plane I could handle, because planes couldn't crash into trees. But I was adamant about cars: I would never get into one again. Luckily Anneke and Jan began to change their lifestyle so it wasn't a problem. I was fine with bikes, buses, trains, and planes.

I knew my parents were dead from the moment my angel held me in his arms. When a doctor at the hospital told me later that my parents were seriously wounded and that "they could not come and see me" I knew that he had meant "never" instead of "not."

Much later Anneke came to tell me that my parents had died. But she didn't say *died*, she said *passed away*.

Everyone kept saying that I was lucky to be alive, but those first years without my parents there were times when I didn't want to keep on living. Sometimes I wished for another accident, with Anneke, Jan, and me, and that I would be the one who died, to set everything to rights again.

We were on that flight from Greece when I finally began to talk about the accident. We had arrived late at the check-in counter, and we hadn't gotten good seats. Jan was sitting alone in one row, and Anneke and I were sitting together behind him. Soon after we took off, Jan fell asleep with his head leaning a little toward the seat next to him. I looked at his hair between the seat backs and I kept telling myself his name was Jan. His hair was dirty blond, like my father's. Anneke wanted to talk and pointed out the window at the view. I glanced out the window and decided I didn't want to talk about the landscape.

"The last time I saw my father, I saw his hair against the back of a seat. The same way I see Jan's hair now." Anneke looked at me in surprise. "I saw his hair and my mother's too. I was sitting in the backseat of the car and the radio was on. I fell asleep. Then I never saw them again. Not alive, not dead."

"It's better to remember them alive, sweetie, it was such a terrible accident . . ."

"I woke up in a hospital bed."

"I know, sweetie, you don't have to talk about it if you don't want to."

I had kept my silence for over four years. I wanted to talk, I wanted to make her uncomfortable by telling her everything that had happened to me. Most importantly I wanted her to understand that my mother was still here, despite the fact that Anneke had taken her place.

"I woke up in a hospital bed. There was a girl sitting next to my bed who wasn't my mother."

"It was the girl who saw the accident. She just happened to be riding past on her bike. She called the ambulance and then she went to the hospital. She stayed in your room for a few hours. But when Jan and I arrived she had left."

I knew. I knew everything that had happened.

"She was there when I woke up, and then I never saw her again."

"She must have been tired from riding her bike so far, poor girl. She had already done so much, she probably wanted to go home." Anneke was searching for words, as if she could help me. But she couldn't. "It was very important that she ride to Someren-Eind as fast as she could to raise the alarm. Thanks to her the ambulance arrived just in time to get you out of the car."

"The ambulance was late," I said angrily.

"You're right. It was too late for your parents, but the girl couldn't pedal any faster, and it arrived in time to save you."

"No, the ambulance was too late for me, too."

She furrowed her brow.

"Before the ambulance arrived, there was a boy," I explained. "He was an angel. He got me out of the car. When the ambulance arrived, the car was already a ball of flames."

That night I heard Anneke and Jan talking in their bedroom. Anneke was softly saying that I had been so traumatized by the accident that I had invented an angel.

They didn't know. They didn't know that apart from the girl on the bike there was a boy who had saved me and held me until the ambulance arrived. I knew. And my body knew, though I couldn't remember anything between when I fell asleep in the car and when I woke up in hospital. I had no memories, I just had the conviction that a real-life angel had come, and that my parents were dead.

The next day I told Anneke that I wanted to go to Someren, that I wanted to find the angel and the girl. Anneke said that sounded good and we set a date to visit.

We took one of the first trains of the day to Helmond and then we took a bus to Someren. On the way there I thought how one day long ago I had taken the same journey, there and back, with my parents on the way there, and on the way back in an ambulance that had taken me from Someren to the hospital in Helmond.

The bus left the N226 before we passed *the place*. We got out in the center of Someren, in front of the town hall. I was happy because I had decided that was where they'd know the most about the residents of Someren. Anneke suggested that we have a cup of tea and some apple pie in a café first, to rest from the journey, and I agreed because I needed to use the toilet.

While we were eating the apple pie Anneke tried to prepare me for disappointment.

"You know, they might not be able to help you, sweetie, okay?"

"That's alright, Anneke." I was a child and I was cruel. I liked calling her by her first name so that people would realize she wasn't my real mother.

"Have you considered the possibility that the girl on the bike wasn't from around here?"

I didn't answer. I didn't say anything else.

We walked in silence to the town hall. There weren't many people around, and it looked like they might be about to close, so I hurried to one of the counters.

"Do you know anything about a serious car accident that happened here four years ago?" I asked resolutely.

"A car accident? Unfortunately we have lots of car accidents every ye . . ." The woman paused for a moment, looked at Anneke, who was standing behind me, and looked back at me. Suddenly her face clouded over. "Are you talking about the accident on the highway between Someren and Someren -Eind? A couple with a little girl?"

"Yes!" I said excitedly. "Do you know anything about the people who saved the girl?"

"Uh, the ambulance crew?"

"No," I said sharply. "The boy who got there before the ambulance, and the girl who called the ambulance."

"Well, young lady, no, I didn't know there was a boy."

Anneke butted into our conversation.

"He was an angel, that boy, a real life angel," she said slowly, emphasizing the word *angel*. I saw her wink at the woman. "The angel is the one who really saved her, not the ambulance crew."

"Oh, I see, an angel."

"What about the girl on the bike?" I asked, to get the town official's attention back.

"The girl . . . wasn't from around here. I remember her saying how lucky it was that she happened to be riding past right then. But she wasn't from around here. She witnessed the accident, rode to Someren-Eind as quickly as she could, asked someone to call an ambulance, and left again in a hurry."

"She was also at the hospital," I said, sounding a little like a know-it-all.

"I didn't know that." She knew a lot less than I had expected.

"Thank you," Anneke said to end the conversation. But the woman wasn't quite ready to say good-bye.

"Once in a while we still talk about that awful day here in town. I'm happy to know that the little girl is alright." She moved her hand as if to caress my hair, but I didn't let her.

"I'm not that girl," I said abruptly. "I'm doing some research for a school project. About angels."

"Oh, sorry, I thought it was you." She winked at Anneke.

"I need some information for my research," I continued. "Could you give me a list of everyone who was between the ages of fourteen and fifteen in Someren in the year 1987?"

"A list from the town census? The census only has the names of people who live here."

"The people who were on holiday in Someren at that time too."

"Those people aren't in the town records. There's no way of knowing who they were."

The woman thought for a moment and added, "Now that you mention it, that year there was a tourist campground on the south side of town. Maybe the girl was chaperoning a group of children . . ."

Finally she was taking me seriously, I thought triumphantly.

"But I'm sorry, I can't give you a list," she continued, in the same tone as before. "The names of people who live here are private information. I can only give a list like that to the police, if they request one, of course, and they need to have a really good reason for asking."

I didn't believe her.

"We understand," Anneke said behind me. I turned and looked at her, infuriated. Why did she have to take sides with the woman, when she should be on mine? She should have tried to convince the woman how important the list was to me. "You know what?" Anneke said in an unfortunate, maternal tone of voice.

"What?" I said angrily.

"Let's go to the church. Pastors always know lots of things about their congregations. Maybe he'll be able to help us."

"That's a very good idea," the town official said. Now she was happy to see us leave.

"No. Let's go to the police," I said emphatically.

So we went to the police. Anneke walked along beside me, worried. At the police station, an officer told me in a babyish voice that they only had lists of bad people, not angels. I told him that I wasn't a little girl, that he could speak to me like an adult, because I had been through a lot in my life.

"My parents died when I was eight," I said gravely. His expression changed. Now I had his attention. "I don't want you to make me a list, I want you ask the lady in the town hall to give me one. If you ask her, she'll give it to you, but if I ask her, she won't."

"Ah, now I see," the officer said.

He didn't say he would. And he didn't say he wouldn't. He smiled at me and I quickly took a piece of paper and a pen from his desk and wrote down Anneke and Jan's address.

"When you get the list, you can send it to this address."

"But you know I can't do that, right?" he insisted.

"Just in case you can."

"Okay." He took the piece of paper with the address and held it in his hand.

"Thank you very much," Anneke said. "It's time to go, sweetie. This man will do everything he can but he might not be able to get a list for you, he has to catch thieves and things like that, you know?"

"He doesn't have to make the list himself, Anneke, he just has to request the list and post it. That's not so hard. It won't take much time at all."

"He'll do what he can, okay? Now it's time for us to go, we told Jan we'd be home soon . . ."

"Don't forget to ask for the names of the older kids from the tourists' campground, they should be on the list, too," I said to the officer. "And thank you very much, sir. Now we can go," I said sharply to Anneke.

On the train Anneke was silent. I was happy.

Two months later a folded sheet of paper without an envelope came through the mail slot. I picked it up, opened it, and read the heading: *One Hundred People*. Beneath the heading was a list of one hundred names and surnames, in four columns of twenty-five.

Him

It was midday on a Friday when, walking back to work after lunch with Willemien, I passed something unusual that gave me the little push I needed. That day, near the Plaza del Comercio, I crossed paths with a couple from abroad who asked me, dictionary in hand, where to find the Dalí Museum. I noticed the woman was enjoying a chocolate bar from the Dutch supermarket Albert Heijn, and I told them the address in my best Dutch. They were so surprised that I had to give them the directions several times, because the first few times they were still processing the fact that I had spoken to them in their own language.

That afternoon I wondered why a Dutch couple would come all the way to Spain just to see the Dalí Museum, when I, who had been in Figueres for four months, hadn't even stopped to take a look at the façade of the building. I knew where the building was but I couldn't even tell them where the main entrance lay.

At the end of the workday, since I was still wondering, I decided to go to the museum and have a look at the building. When I got to the plaza where the entrance was I realized that visitors were still going in and that it was open for another hour. So I bought a ticket.

I had no idea what I was getting myself into. And I felt similarly when I left, not having fully digested what I had seen. I returned home beneath a blackened sky, my perspective of the city around me altered by what I had seen in the museum. In the world of Dalí, things were not what they seemed: a sofa was a woman's lips, but those lips were also a red sofa; balls floating against a sky-blue background were also a woman's face. I thought of the kind of dreams in which things change shape. I thought of Willemien's stone houses, and I knew I had to do whatever it took to get her to the museum as soon as possible. I knew it would make her feel better. With any luck she might even start painting again.

When I got home I could see from Willemien's expression that she expected an explanation for my delay. So I told her I had been inside the Dalí Museum, and that I wanted to do whatever I could to help her see it soon. I remember her smile, her excitement about this plan, but I also remember the sadness in her eyes when, out of the blue, she told me that she could never leave the house again. Her look of fear and powerlessness broke my heart. Those eyes gave me the incentive to make a permanent change the following Monday.

I got to the shop before my boss and waited for him at the door. He was surprised to see me so early but he realized there was something important I wanted to discuss with him, because he opened the security screen, but he only raised it halfway, making it clear to any potential customers that we weren't open yet. We bent down and entered the shop, took two chairs from the shop floor, and sat down amongst the televisions and VCRs.

"What happened?" he asked, looking at me in a way he never had before.

"Nothing happened. I just want to explain my situation to you."

"How's your wife doing?"

I had been working in the shop for months and I had never mentioned my wife, not once. Willemien had hardly left the house, and naïve as I am, I had convinced myself that no one knew she existed. The truth is that I didn't want people to get to know Willemien as she was now, I wanted to wait for the old Willemien to return, to introduce strong, healthy Willemien to the world. I didn't want anyone's sympathy, for her or for me. But when my boss asked me if my wife was okay it dawned on me. I realized that in a town like Figueres, after living there for a few months, everyone knows what's going on in your home. The kids would have talked about it at school, the woman at the market would have had her suspicions when I asked for some chicory, and the checkout girl at the supermarket would have realized it when I bought sanitary towels for Willemien.

On the one hand I felt as if a huge secret had been suddenly exposed, but on the other I knew that being able to talk about it was for the best. So I told my boss what I had been thinking of telling him.

"My wife is the same as usual, I think she's gotten a little better since we arrived from Holland, but she still doesn't want to go outside. We'll have to start sometime, though she worries about going out when the streets are busy, not that she's avoiding people. She needs to have contact with someone besides me and the children, she still hasn't met anyone here, though she's always been quite social." I stopped talking for a moment, worked up my courage, and eventually said, "What I want to ask you is . . . I mean, what we need is . . . I'd like to take her to the Dalí Museum one day, but on a weekday, because there would be less visitors and we'd be more comfortable."

There it was, I'd said it. My hands were sweating, I was afraid some customer would poke his head under the security gate to see if we were open yet, I was afraid that my boss would say I couldn't take a day off until August. I was afraid that if he turned down my request, I'd have to quit working for him. But I didn't need to be afraid of anything.

"A few days ago I was speaking with my wife," he said. "Years ago my mother-in-law was living with us when she was ill. She never went out, but she had family and friends who would come and visit her in the afternoon sometimes. Time passed more pleasantly that way. I think there are people who don't like to see anyone when they're bedridden, but there are others who need to see their loved ones. What I mean is that my wife was asking whether your wife is having a hard time, being alone here without relatives and friends to visit her. No one knows what's going on, but my wife was offering to visit your wife. I know that doesn't have anything to do with your question, but for the past two weeks I've been wondering whether I should mention it to you or not. As far as taking a day off to go to the museum, anytime is fine."

I was speechless. I realized how difficult we can make things for ourselves when we don't have the nerve to say what we're thinking or what's going on. We fill our lives with conjecture and supposition, which we base our actions on, and in the end they're false assumptions.

Our conversation that Monday morning changed many things. I felt that Willemien and I weren't alone in what we were going through, because there was a whole community around us, which cared about us and wanted to see us triumph.

That Thursday we went out to see if we could make it to the Dalí Museum. Our plan was just to go and look at the building, to have a seat on one of the benches if she needed to rest, and return home. In the morning I went to work but I finished earlier than usual so we could have an early lunch. We left the house at two in the afternoon. It was a quiet time of day, because the shops were shut and the neighbors were all at home eating.

We walked out the door of our building into a gorgeous May afternoon. The streets smelled like spring and the blue sky was dotted with little clouds that looked like the eyes through which it was watching us.

Willemien held my arm as we walked, carefully observing the façades of the houses, the stones in the pavement, and the clothes of the few people with whom we crossed paths. When we arrived at the museum plaza, instead of sitting down, she felt like she wanted to keep going. If the museum had been open right then, there's no doubt we would have gone in. But it was fine to leave it for another day, too. That way we could make another plan, there was something to look forward to, to keep us going.

In the afternoon I returned to work and told my boss about our small victory. And from that day forward there were more and more victories in our adventure. The following week we went to visit the museum, inside; we were there for two hours and we only saw half of it, because Willemien could spend ages staring at a painting or a sculpture. At one point during our visit I asked her if it made her feel like taking up painting again, but she said definitely not, that she needed to find a new way to express what was percolating in her mind. I realized that we'd had this conversation a few years earlier, and that she was still convinced she was finished with canvas. I tried to imagine what she would do instead of painting and shuddered when I remembered the artist who had emptied the bottle of lemonade into the North Sea. I hoped Willemien would find a less extravagant way of expressing her creativity. I continued to hope that she'd return to painting, but it was pointless. When Willemien put her mind to something, she didn't change it lightly. And although I didn't believe her at the time, it was true: she never touched her paintbrushes again.

Maria, my boss's wife, was waiting for us at the museum exit. She walked us home and offered to come over the following morning, to keep Willemien company.

Little by little things began to change, Maria's visits became more frequent, and sometimes she even convinced Willemien to go outside for a little while. Eventually the time came when, ten months after our arrival in Figueres, Willemien would go out on her own, and only went to bed when it was time to go to sleep.

We celebrated the anniversary of our arrival in Cataluña by buying a flat. Willemien said we needed a change, to leave her illness behind in the bed in the flat we had rented, to take another step toward winning this game. The apartment was on Moreria Street; it was January 1978 when we moved in.

That first night in our new home, sick Willemien got into bed and the old Willemien got out of it. She often went out to visit the Dalí Museum, to meet Maria for a walk and a chat, or to take the boys to the Toy Museum, where Robert and Simon, who were seven and ten, felt like they were living a dream, and Arjen, who had grown up quickly in the past year, tried his best to pretend he was not bored to death.

It wasn't long after these museum visits began that Willemien started to write. She began with the story of the stone houses. She showed me her story and I was delighted to return to the fantasy she had first invented visiting my homeland. Then she told me she was working on a new project but that I couldn't ask her anything about it until she had finished. So I didn't. A few weeks later she showed me what she had written.

It wasn't a story. It was much larger than a sheet of paper, practically a poster, a broad white background broken only by small words scattered in space, connected by fine lines. Before I realized what I was looking at I already had a name for it. It was a constellation. I took a close look at the tiny words and I saw that each of them was a name. In the center I found my name, and Willemien's, accompanied by the children's. Around us, a little further away, were the names of my boss, Carles, and his wife, Maria, the woman at the market-stall, Pepita, and Arjen's teacher, Teresa. In total there were about twenty names that made up our world, the people around us who we had gotten to know since we moved to Figueres. There was still a lot of blank space around these twenty names, space that would be occupied by the other people we'd meet as we proceeded on our journey.

"Arjen's first girlfriend," Willemien said, smiling, "the assistant who will work in our shop when we open it, my first student in my painting classes, everyone will have a place in this constellation, they will all be connected to us."

I looked at the poster for a long time, wondering why Willemien needed to fill a blank piece of paper with the names of our friends and acquaintances. As if she had read my mind she said, "I made it so we won't forget we're not alone."

The good years arrived. Willemien insisted she needed a bicycle to get around town. I didn't like the idea, it seemed dangerous to me, there were more cars on the road every day, and because in Spain only children rode bicycles around town. I still remember my last conversation with Willemien about this, her vehemence and her reasoning. She needed to get around town easily, she said, she needed to feel the wind on her face, to feel a little bit Dutch. And all of this could be accomplished by buying a bicycle. It was so simple, but all I could think about was what people would say. Then she said it, she spat out one of those phrases she knew would put an end to the discussion: "Why is it that in Holland you never worried about what the neighbors would say when the children were still awake having dinner at nine at night?"

We bought a white Orbea bicycle. Willemien put some colorful stripes on it with electrical tape, to personalize it, and began riding around town. In the beginning the neighbors watched her, surprised, but soon Willemien and her bicycle were accepted as part of the Figueran landscape. When we opened a small painting school a year later, almost everyone in town knew the teacher was the cyclist with the foreign accent.

The school worked out well. Willemien had students to keep her busy and to lavish her creativity upon.

We never did open the electronic appliance store that Willemien had envisioned. We didn't need to. We were happy, I in my job and she in her school, the boys growing up, playing in the streets, studying in high school and making plans for the future.

Life carried on. One by one the boys left; Arjen to Holland, and Simon and Robert to Barcelona. Things happened the way they were meant to, and we survived what had been thrust upon us. Until we couldn't any longer. Until she passed away.

Her

A plane was zooming overhead when I walked into Karen Abrams's bar.

"Have you heard?" Karen Abrams asked me, upset.

"About what?"

"They want to demolish an entire town."

"What?"

"Some no-name town in Groningen, they've decided they don't need it anymore, this town, and they want to turn it into a nature preserve. Turning it back over to nature. How ridiculous is that?"

"I don't know the details, but it doesn't sound so strange to me. If no one lives there anymore, it seems like a good idea."

"Yeah, but people do still live there! That's why it's scandalous! People who chose to live in a quiet little town and along come the city-folk and say, *Look, a little town like this, no one wants to live here, it's too quiet . . . Hey, let's get rid of it.*"

"You know someone from there?"

"No, not a soul. But I do know those young politicians who think they'll go a long way proposing crazy ideas like this."

I didn't have any interest in continuing the conversation. The truth was that I couldn't have cared less what happened to the town. If Karen Abrams had heard about it, on the news no doubt, then there were already plenty of people on the case. I didn't need to get involved, too.

I was unmoved by her indignation. She stood there expectantly and I looked out the window.

"What are you thinking about?" she eventually asked me.

"I agreed to be interviewed about my hundred names. Do you remember what I told you?"

"Yeah, the journalist with the Spanish surname."

"I agreed to meet her here. She'll be here in half an hour. I didn't want to meet her at my place. You never know what a journalist might write . . ."

"Here? Don't you think it's too busy? Wouldn't you rather go upstairs and do it in my kitchen?"

Now that she mentioned it, that did seem like a better place to meet—the place where I had begun my search.

"Do you want to go get ready? Have a think about what you want to tell her? You have to be careful with journalists, they know exactly what to ask to get the answers they want to hear," Karen Abrams said.

I nodded and she said she'd take me up.

"I can help you get ready." She arranged for someone to watch the bar and for someone to bring Lianne Pérez-Horst upstairs, when she came, and we went upstairs to her living room. She tidied up a little while I looked around, trying to imagine what Lianne Pérez-Horst would see. Karen Abrams's home was the exact opposite of the journalist's. Instead of parquet floors, this one had wall-to-wall carpeting; instead of tall bookshelves, Karen Abrams had a jungle of plants. Instead of cats, this old building had mice.

I decided to make sure Lianne Pérez-Horst knew this wasn't my home.

I looked at the time on my phone. In twenty minutes everything would change. Karen Abrams made two cups of tea and we sat at the same table in the same seats where we'd sat when I asked her that first time we met about Someren. The only difference was that now we were surrounded by winter's feeble light and the room looked smaller. I realized I was seeing the real Karen Abrams, not the barkeep. Two years had passed, and I still knew nothing about her. Perhaps she had a few more wrinkles, but apart from that she was still the same svelte, frail woman I had met back then. I only saw this side of her in her living room. The other side of her, the one I saw downstairs, always hid her body behind the bar, making her seem stronger and older.

"I'll leave you alone when she gets here," Karen Abrams said after I looked at my phone for a third time. I knew she would have liked to stay. She went downstairs and a few minutes later Lianne Pérez-Horst appeared. I was looking out the window; I didn't expect her quite so soon.

The journalist approached me, smiling. She carried an impressive backpack for her photography equipment, which she quickly opened on the kitchen table. She took out a small microphone, a pair of cables, a tape recorder, and a camera. She glanced around as she set the equipment up on the table.

I sat down in front of the microphone and realized she had chosen the seat that gave me a view of the whole room. I hadn't realized before: it was obviously the "visitor's seat" with the best view—if there was a good view in the place. Lianne Pérez-Horst sat down in the chair facing the kitchen. With a little luck, or not, she might even see a mouse scamper across the counter.

"Karen Abrams has been kind enough to let us meet up here," I said just to make it clear that if a mouse did appear, it wasn't my mouse.

"Yes, it's very kind of her." Lianne Pérez-Horst was still busy testing her equipment. She finally sat down in front of me.

"Okay, let's begin," she said. She turned the tape recorder on, waited a few seconds, and asked, "Would you like to tell me about your list of one hundred names?"

Suddenly it all seemed like a bad idea. Somehow I had expected her to start by saying something about why we were doing the interview, before throwing the first question at me. Now I felt like I was trapped in a live broadcast. The tape recorder intimidated me. If I said too much, if I said something slightly inaccurate, I wouldn't be able to take it back. Everything would be recorded on that machine so she could listen to it over and over again.

Lianne Pérez-Horst waited for me to answer but I didn't know where to begin. I didn't want to talk about the day when Anneke and I had gone to the Someren town hall and police station to request the list. Although everything had happened just as I remembered it, I knew the story sounded completely absurd.

"They sent it to my house," I eventually said.

"Who sent it?"

"Someone who wanted to help me."

"Someone who knows who you're looking for?"

"I don't think the person who sent the list knows. They just supplied a list of the likely candidates."

"How did they decide which names should be on the list?"

"I don't know."

The doubts. The same doubts I'd always harbored, she had them too. The possibility the list was the result of a misunderstanding, or that Anneke had made it, or that I had made it. Nevertheless, I had always wanted to believe that the police officer had sent me the list; was there really any other option for him? I needed to believe this, like a lie I had decided to accept. As a secret.

There's no such thing as a life without secrets. Couples have secrets, families have secrets, cities have secrets, countries have secrets. I have my own secrets. But it's also a fact that sooner or later, secrets come to light.

"One day I folded the list with the hundred names into a paper plane," I said into the microphone. "I threw the plane into the garden of Anneke and Jan's house for a reason: if it fell in the pond, and the list sank slowly into the water, it would be a sign that I had to forget about it, that the list was stupid. But if it didn't, if the plane landed on the grass, it would be a sign it was real, a sign not to give up. If the plane landed on the grass, I would begin searching for my angel."

Lianne Pérez-Horst wrote the names "Jan" and "Anneke" in her notebook of graph paper.

"You put your fate in the hands of the wind?" she asked, while her pen made a question mark after Anneke's name.

"I was fifteen."

"Did you have to fish the plane out of the pond?"

"It landed on the grass."

I sat there, silent. She held her pen still.

"After launching the plane," I continued, "I ran down to the garden to get the list, before Anneke and Jan saw what I was doing. Then I unfolded the paper and I reread all the names on the list until I had memorized them. From that moment on, I knew I would find them all, though I still didn't know how. I also thought it was possible I might run into the people on the list at any time. So I needed to memorize them, so I'd always know."

"Would you recite the names on the list for me?"

"Why? I can show you."

"I'd like to hear you say them."

I don't know why I did it. Perhaps because I wanted her to like me.

"Karen Abrams," I began, reciting slowly, "Anke Adriaans," it sounded like I was taking attendance. "Henk Bakermans ... Ana Mei Balau ... Robert Bayens ... Paul Jan Blauw ... Fritz Boertjes ... Maria G. Bongers ... Jasper Bouwmans ... Hans Brinkman ... Dan van den Broek ... Jenny Bruijstens ... Daphne van Bussel ... Sander Castelijns ... Femke Castillo ... Ellen H. Croese ... Ineke Crooijmans ... Joost Derkx ... Willem Díaz ... Tracy van Diepen ..."

I stopped.

"That should give you an idea," I said, to stop her from asking me to continue.

"How many of them have you spoken with?"

"About eighty, I think."

"In other words you're nearly at the end of the list?"

"No. Sometimes I find more than one person with the same name. And some of the people have referred me to others, to people who aren't on my list, but I visited them anyway because they had a connection to the town."

"And you still haven't found anyone who can tell you anything about the accident?"

"Not specifically, but many of them have connections to Someren, they have relatives there, they lived there themselves, or they still do. Some of them remember the news and the talk in town the days after the accident. But I haven't found anyone who witnessed it."

"And what have you found?"

"What do you mean?"

"I imagine you've talked to lots of people. All sorts of people. I'm wondering if you've seen their homes, if they've told you about their lives. It seems to me that it must be fascinating to get to know all those people, telling them your story and seeing how they react."

"I guess it may seem fascinating to you, but there's nothing fascinating about it to me. For me it's a huge blow every time I ring a doorbell and meet someone who can't help me."

Lianne Pérez-Horst seemed disappointed by my reply. I thought she didn't understand the gravity of my search. She thought the mystery of these hundred names was more important than my need to find the person who had saved me. It was understandable. All she knew was that there had been an accident. She didn't know how dramatically it had altered my life. Only I knew that.

She recorded my voice for three hours. She got more and more excited and eventually she decided she also needed to speak to Karen Abrams. That was fine with me. I went downstairs to get her and she told her version of the day I first walked into her bar.

Before leaving, Lianne Pérez-Horst took a picture of Karen Abrams and me at a table in the bar. She said she'd let me see the article before she published it. She was already in the street when she realized that she had only meant to take a picture of the list.

She left with a little piece of my life in her hands.

Him

In 1995 I flew to Holland to bury Willemien in her country. It was a very difficult journey. Just three months earlier we had flown to Holland for the birth of our Arjen's first daughter. Willemien wasn't feeling one hundred percent, but she wanted to meet her granddaughter and nothing and no one, not even I, was going to come between her and the little one. The trip was fine, I saw that Willemien was very happy, but also that the hustle and bustle of traveling and the cold weather in Holland weakened her.

Without Willemien, I couldn't hold the girl. I didn't want to. I know it wasn't her fault, but I was afraid of the loneliness I would feel when I held her, since Willemien couldn't hold her, too. I told Arjen I needed time, and he understood. Luckily he did, because I didn't. I was afraid of my own thoughts. In some corner of my mind I thought that if the baby hadn't been born, and we hadn't visited her three months earlier, Willemien would have lived a few more weeks, or even months. I was tortured by the idea, and I couldn't get over it until I eventually realized that even if our granddaughter hadn't been born, Willemien would have wanted to go to Holland. Because she already knew that it would be her final visit.

After the burial, Simon and Robert tried to talk me into moving to Barcelona, to live with one of them. I declined, I didn't want to impede upon their lives, and I preferred to return to Extremadura.

It had been a long time since I had traveled to my village by train, and with such a small suitcase. That trip was like going back in time. It didn't occur to me beforehand that without my car I'd have to get around town walking, alone, like I did in my youth. The only thought in my head was that I didn't want to travel a thousand kilometers by car without Willemien at my side.

I brought Willemien's wooden box along, as if it were a substitute for her.

When I arrived, after traveling for more than twenty-four hours straight, Antonia was waiting for me, to drive me to the village in her car. After all those years, my sister still looked at me like I was her hero, and I preferred to be welcomed as a hero than as an interloper, which is why it was her I told I was coming, instead of Pedro.

Of course, Pedro was also waiting for me when we got to my parents' old house. Now it was Antonia's house, and that day Mariana was in the kitchen making stew for lunch, which we would all share—brothers, sisters, brothers-in-law, sisters-in-law, nephews, and nieces. I don't know how many of us there were that day, they took me completely by surprise; what I do know is that I missed Willemien and our three sons terribly.

Empty hours, empty days passed. I didn't know what to do with all those minutes, those seconds. I walked around, watching other people living their lives, as if mine had ceased.

Until one day I suddenly realized that I didn't belong there.

After a personal tragedy we make critical decisions on the spur of the moment but they're often temporary because they're driven by emotions that are still raw. The certainty I had felt when I decided to start a new life in my hometown disappeared without a trace.

One bright, silent morning I decided that there was nothing wrong with changing my mind. I had been at Antonia's house for two weeks, I had felt loved and cared for, but I needed to find my own path. Unsure of what I would do next, I decided to leave the path I had chosen and go to Barcelona to visit Simon. But I didn't call him beforehand; I thought I'd call from the station in Barcelona. I wanted to travel in peace, without knowing that someone would be waiting for me at the other end of my journey. I'd sleep in a narrow bunk, listening to the rhythm of the wheels turning around and around on their axes without hearing them. My body would feel the ground covering distance beneath me, leaving my past further and further behind.

Things never turn out quite the way we expect them to. What's important is to know what your goal is. I wanted to begin a new life somewhere pleasant, leaving my recent past in another pleasant place behind, to be able to enjoy my memories of Willemien without the grief of losing her too soon. In the end I achieved my goal, it took me months of traveling paths I never would have imagined traveling, but I did manage to find peace again.

Antonia accompanied me to Cáceres; I took the train to Madrid, where I waited for the Talgo. I had reserved a private sleeper compartment, just as I had on my outward journey, because I had no desire whatsoever to sleep next to a stranger. When I boarded the train I was greeted by a steward in a blue uniform who looked like he had just gotten out of bed. The young man had just arisen because he had to work all night, and his fresh face was welcoming despite its contrast to the dark night enveloping us. The steward had a name tag pinned to his chest: *Roberto*. Although they had the same name, he bore no resemblance at all to our Robert, no doubt because his mother wasn't Dutch. This thought promptly made me wonder whether his mother and father were still alive, or if he'd already had to bid one of them good-bye.

"Good evening," Roberto said, sounding a little rehearsed. "May I see your ticket please?"

I searched my jacket pockets for the ticket and, as is always the case, I found it in the last one I checked. I handed it to him and he smiled when he read it.

"Thank you very much. Come with me, please. Your companion just arrived a few minutes ago," he said guilelessly, and he turned into the carriage corridor. My feet were frozen to the floor.

"Companion? What companion? You must be mistaken, young man," I said, taken aback. "I'm travelling alone."

He looked me up and down a few times and smiled in a remarkably familiar way without saying a word. I immediately recognized that smile. It triggered an avalanche of memories from Holland. Searching through images, faces, and names, I came to the conclusion that the smile I had just seen was the very same one I had seen day after day on the face of one of my roommates in Someren, long ago. It turned out that the steward for my carriage was the son of Paco, the liveliest of our group of eight, the one who never stopped talking once he got started, who suffered from insomnia and could make the nights unbearable by keeping you awake if he couldn't sleep. The last I had heard of him was that after eight years in Holland he had returned to Extremadura to continue his life with his wife and children who had waited for him all that time. It had been more than twenty-five years since I had seen Paco.

Roberto accompanied me to my compartment, knocked on the door and an old man opened, exclaiming, "Long time no see!"

"Paco! You haven't changed!" I lied, I couldn't help it.

"You have! You look more Dutch than ever!" he said, lying too.

"What are you doing here? Are you going to Barcelona?"

"Not really. I called Antonia yesterday 'cause I heard you were back in town, and she told me that you were leaving today. We live in Madrid now and I have connections on the Talgo, so I decided to come by before you left. Oh, and I'm really sorry to hear about your wife."

"Thanks. It was hard, but I'm getting used to it," I continued to lie; I needed time to get used to the fact I was talking to a friend. Was he really a friend? We had lived under the same roof and worked in the same factory for years, but did we have anything else in common? He had shown up on the train as if we were bosom buddies. I would never have done that. Perhaps I had made more of an impression on him back then than he had made on me. Perhaps he had idealized his years in the camp and the factory after his early return to Spain. Or perhaps we had been good friends and I had simply forgotten.

Roberto departed, saying that the train would be leaving in a quarter of an hour. Fifteen minutes with an old acquaintance, I thought. But Paco had other plans. He spent the fifteen minutes telling me what had happened in his life over the past twenty-five years and, since he didn't make any sign of leaving, I asked him if he ought to be getting on.

"Don't worry," he said enthusiastically, "I can always go to Barcelona and return tomorrow on another Talgo." I shuddered at the thought of spending the night with this man who I still had not fully reconciled with the young man from Extremadura I had known in Holland. "It'll be like old times, in our bunk beds in Someren. Remember?"

I looked at the bunks in the compartment—my compartment—, which were folded up to make four seats; I couldn't see any resemblance with the beds in our Dutch camp. I didn't want to think of those bunks in Someren, I didn't want to remember the bed where I had dreamed of a beautiful life with Willemien night after night. Thirty years had passed, that dream had become a reality, and then the dream had died.

How do you remember a dream that, once you've accomplished it, dies too soon? Willemien would have known how to answer that question. But now that it had occurred to me to ask her, Willemien was dead, and I was aboard a train with a young man grown old.

Paco didn't leave when the whistle sounded, or when the train doors shut, or when the train lurched forward. The man kept talking and talking, until he asked, "So, tell me! How did Holland treat you?"

Luckily I didn't have to answer because Roberto came in and asked us if we'd like to join him in the bar car. His father didn't hesitate, he got up and insisted I join them.

In the restaurant car there was a bottle of wine waiting for us, which Paco poured. Then he raised his glass in a toast: "To returning to our roots, to Extremadura," he said, his eyes shining.

"To roots," I said through my teeth. What roots, I thought. The ones I put down in the village, the ones I put down in Holland, or the ones I put down these last few years in Figueres—the ones I've decided to leave behind so as not to run into Willemien every time I turn the corner?

Roberto waved to a stewardess who had just entered the restaurant car. She came over and said hello to Paco, too. While Paco made small talk with the young woman, Roberto explained to me that his father often joined him on the shifts he was working. He had retired early due to back problems and he got bored staying at home. So Roberto invited him along whenever he knew the train wasn't too full.

We spent hours in the restaurant car. After a while we stopped talking, though I hadn't been so talkative myself, and began playing with some dominos Paco had brought along. Roberto disappeared temporarily at every station to see if anyone was boarding or disembarking, then he'd return to join us.

At three in the morning Paco went to bed and I decided to stay up a half hour longer. Not that I wasn't tired, I was completely exhausted, but I thought I'd sleep better if I waited a little, to be certain that when I went to bed there wasn't an ex-emigrant from Extremadura under my bunk, asking me what I had been up to lately.

That half hour in the restaurant car without Paco became hours, and it changed my destination. I don't know how it happened, but I found myself talking to Roberto about his experiences on the train, of his life as a train steward and his way of understanding where people came from.

"I'm Extremaduran, my family is Extremaduran, and I've never lived abroad, but I'm the son of an emigrant,"

Roberto said. "I can't escape that fact. My father went to live at the opposite end of the earth for years, leaving my mother alone and pregnant. You know that back in the sixties anything beyond Spain's borders was the other end of the earth. Sometimes he showed up at the holidays and then he went away again. I was conceived during one of those holidays. I think that's why I had to look so long to find out where I belonged, and I finally found it when I boarded the Talgo.

A few thoughts had occurred to me, but Roberto didn't seem interested in my opinion. He really was his father's son.

"I think some people are rooted in themselves," he continued. Once in a while he looked at me to make sure I was still awake. "When you're rooted in yourself, you feel settled wherever you go. I guess to feel good we need to find places to adapt to. Except once we've adapted we need to move on, to find a new place to adapt to. But once you've adapted to several different places, you no longer have one place where you belong. That's when the place where you belong becomes the space between those two different places. Moving around and seeing new places—that's my natural habitat. The truth is I'm a nomad."

He fell silent. It seemed like this was the first time in his life he had voiced these thoughts. These words had been dancing in his head for years, but he had never said them aloud. In the chaos of his monologue, there was something that had caught my attention, a familiar conclusion. Perhaps I was a nomad, too, perhaps my third life—the years in Figueres—had made me become rootless, too.

Maybe it was because it was four in the morning, but the fact of the matter is that I finally began to talk.

"I'm a nomad, too," I said, choosing my words much more carefully than he had. "I don't have roots anywhere in the world, but at the same time I have roots everywhere. Part of me is in Extremadura, part of me is in Holland, and part of me is in Cataluña." I drew three spaces on the table with my hands. The three spaces were separate, forming a triangle. Extremadura was on the left, twenty centimeters in front of me, Holland was in the middle, about fifty centimeters away, and Cataluña was nearer, on the right. They formed an equilateral triangle. I fell silent, wondering where to spend the rest of my life. Eventually I said, "And then there's a huge void."

Roberto drew an arc on the table, through the triangle. Then he said, "The void fills with movement, the void can only be filled by doing things, moving around. Searching."

"For what?"

"Anything. People who are searching have a goal. They have a reason to get up in the morning, they know that eventually they'll find what they're looking for, and they have a reason to live."

"What are you searching for?"

My question caught him off guard.

"I'm not searching for anything."

"You've found everything you were looking for already?"

"No, I mean I'm not looking for anything in particular, I take what comes, I let life surprise me, knowing that whatever happens it will always be good, or at least there will be something good about it. Working on the Talgo, I meet different people and see different things every day, there's always something new to see. For example, when I got up this morning, I never imagined I'd spend the night talking to one of my father's old friends. If I had known, I would have had preconceived notions about what would happen, perhaps I would have decided to leave you alone to let you talk about the past. But since I didn't know, I didn't 'plan' anything, I let whatever's going to happen happen, and that's how you and I have ended up talking here."

I thought about what I would have done if I had known ten minutes before I boarded the train that Paco was waiting for me in my compartment. Maybe I would have stayed in a hotel in Madrid. I would have slept, sad and alone, in my hotel room, and, the next evening I would have slept on the train, sad and alone once more.

"In other words, if I understand what you're saying, we have two options in life: to go searching or to let yourself be surprised," I said, genuinely interested in his opinion.

"They're two different ways of dealing with the present. We generally combine the two, except when we lose heart, then we have to search. In order not to be reminded of what has made us lose heart."

"And you think it's time for me to search now?"

"Only you can answer that question."

Before retiring to my compartment to sleep for the last few hours of the journey, Roberto invited me to join him on the Talgo whenever I wanted. He'd put me in an empty compartment, and after the trip he'd let me sleep in the spare bed in the hotel room where they put him up.

I told him I'd think it over.

Her

It was Saturday morning. I had stayed up talking to Karen Abrams in the bar until all hours and eventually I agreed to stay over and sleep on the sofa in her living room. While she was making coffee, I looked around me, disoriented; her house was beginning to grow on me.

We had breakfast together and then I sat down at her computer to read my emails. Lianne Pérez-Horst had already sent a message with the draft of her article.

It was difficult for me to recognize the woman Lianne Pérez-Horst described. She talked about perseverance and patience. I even read that, according to her, I was "both happy and damaged, at the same time."

She described an endless, romanticized search. It struck me as a movie, not my own life.

"It's your life as she sees it," Karen Abrams said.

"She only met you for three hours, you've known yourself for thirty years."

A staggering thought, one that had never occurred to me.

I sent a reply, giving her my approval. Karen Abrams asked me if I'd like to go into town with her. I said I had things to do. I didn't want to spend too much time in her company.

On the way home Anneke called me. She was in Amsterdam to take care of a few things, she said, and she asked if I had time to go shopping with her. There was no doubt in my mind that, since it was Saturday, Anneke didn't have business to attend to in Amsterdam. She had come just to see me. It seemed like a fine idea to go shopping with her.

At the end of the afternoon we went for a bite to eat. I knew what the dinner would be like. Anneke always looked around in restaurants and bars. She watched people and listened to them. Sometimes eating in a restaurant with her was no different from eating alone, because other people's conversations seemed to interest her more than talking to me. Sometimes it was the same on the bus or the train, but in those cases it seemed like people were more aware of the fact she was eavesdropping, and those conversations seemed to interest her less.

When I was younger I didn't go out to dinner with her as often, so the fact had escaped me. It was only since I'd begun my studies at university, since I'd moved out, that I'd realized it. We were eating in a restaurant and I was telling her something when I noticed her turn her head a little so she could better hear the conversation at the next table. It was so obvious, and it struck me as so embarrassing. I couldn't understand why she found it so interesting.

"It's just a question of coincidence," she said quietly. "It's so interesting to see what we can learn just by listening to the conversations around us. I'm also interested in what you're saying, of course, sweetie, but we've got all night to talk. You can learn so much from the people around you sometimes . . ."

From that point on I realized that seeing Anneke in public was quite different from seeing her at home. In time I got used to it, I didn't find it embarrassing anymore and I even saw it in a positive light. If she was listening to other people, it meant I didn't have her undivided attention, and that made me feel like I had room to breathe.

But that Saturday, after shopping, we sat down to eat at five thirty in an empty restaurant. And she chose a table that was set apart, near the window. The other tables were a few meters away, hidden behind some columns.

At first I thought perhaps Anneke wanted to talk to me about something important, but that wasn't the case. For once she had chosen the window—and my company—over the conversations of strangers. I talked about Jenny and her mood boards again. I knew I had told her before, but I couldn't think of anything else to pass the time. I didn't really have anything else I could tell her about. It was all work-related, or about my search. My job was boring, and my search was a secret.

After the waiter took our order, I noticed Anneke was watching another table. For a moment I thought she was eavesdropping on another conversation. But I was wrong.

"People who eat alone make me sad," she said when she looked at me again. I turned and saw a man eating a large plate of pasta by himself.

"I always eat alone, Anneke," I said.

"Of course, you eat alone at home, but not in a bar or a restaurant, that's what I mean." I eat alone there, too, I thought, but I didn't say so. I didn't want to make her uncomfortable.

Sometimes I wondered if my mother would have become like Anneke if she hadn't died. I grew up with the conviction that she wouldn't have, that my mother was different from Anneke, radically so. But the older I got, the more I realized that the image I had of my mother was based on the perspective of an eight-year-old girl. In my head she was a thirty-two-year-old woman in love with her husband and with her daughter, with me. A woman who lived only for me and who could do no wrong.

Anneke was a mistake from the very start. She wasn't my mother: she was my aunt, who had become my mother. A misunderstanding, an error. I wasn't meant to grow up under her roof. She knew this, too, but she couldn't do anything about it.

Time creates wrinkles, and my mother didn't have wrinkles. Anneke did. The same wrinkles my mother would have gotten, in the same places. After all, they were sisters. If my mother had had the opportunity to get wrinkles, perhaps on a Saturday afternoon after shopping she would have said she felt sorry for people who dine alone. She would likely have felt the same way as her sister. If my mother had lived, maybe I would have never dined alone in a bar and I would have felt sorry for people who dine alone, too.

If my mother were still alive, Anneke would have adopted a little boy and she wouldn't have had to put up with her sister's traumatized daughter.

That Saturday afternoon, sitting with Anneke, I realized something for the first time that I ought to have realized much sooner. I understood that Anneke was my mother, because I didn't have any other. Anneke had brought me up, she had loved me, and she was still alive. Anneke's sister had raised a little girl. But Anneke had been my mother for more than twenty years. And she had never abandoned me.

Maybe it was too late, too late to give something back to Anneke. To say thank you. But I felt she deserved it. For the first time I understood that she had lost much more than I had. I had lost my mother, but she had lost her sister and the opportunity to see herself in a child of her own.

I wanted to say something about what I had just realized, but I didn't know how to put it into words. I wanted her to understand that I didn't want to be a thankless child any longer. I wanted to let her in.

"I have a list of a hundred names," I blurted out. I didn't dare look at her, I was ashamed.

"Come again?"

"I want to tell you about something I've been doing, Anneke . . ." Her name put distance between us, as it always had. For once I didn't want that distance to be there, but there was no alternative: I couldn't suddenly start calling her *mother.* "It's something important, dear Anneke," I added. She looked at me, surprised. I knew that word, dear, had sounded very strange, coming from me. It was a word I seldom used, with her or anyone else. "I know you probably won't believe this," I continued, "but a long time ago I received a list of a hundred names."

"How long ago?"

"Not long after we went to visit the town hall and the police station in Someren."

Anneke looked at me, waiting.

"I kept the list hidden for a long time. Two years ago I began to search for the people whose names are on the list." Her eyes seemed to grow wider with each sentence I uttered. I wasn't entirely sure why she was so stunned: it could be the fact I was telling her a secret, but it also might be sheer disbelief.

I told her everything. The first meeting with Karen Abrams, the internet searches, the trips to other countries, the people I had met, from the strangest to the most boring. I confessed that Jenny wasn't my friend, just someone I had met on one of my trips. Then I told her about my meeting with Lianne Pérez-Horst and the interview.

In the silence that ensued I saw how Anneke's eyes had grown misty, and I hoped she wouldn't burst into tears.

"Thank you," she eventually said.

"For what?"

"For telling me this."

"I should have done it sooner."

"It's always hard to be open with the people we're closest to."

Sometimes silence can make it possible to better understand something you've just heard, and sometimes silence begs to be filled. In the silence that followed, I wanted to ponder Anneke's words, but she decided to fill the void.

"Do you think you'll find what you're looking for?"

"I don't know."

"How do you feel when you meet someone and realize they're not the person you're looking for?"

"Sometimes I feel closer to learning the truth, and sometimes I feel further from it. Sometimes I have no expectations at all." I paused to reflect for a moment before speaking the following words, "It just keeps me busy."

The man who was dining alone was having his coffee and writing something in a notebook. I wondered whether he had been watching us, if he thought we were mother and daughter. I constantly wondered that when Anneke and I were together in public. I kept asking myself if the people around us could tell that we weren't really mother and daughter. I always hoped that people would be able to tell from the distance between us that Anneke was undoubtedly not my mother.

"It might be that you finish your search and realize there was nothing to find," she spoke softly and slowly. "It might be that you need this search to relinquish your dream," she looked at me to see if I reacted, but I didn't. "I'm not saying this boy doesn't exist . . . But you may never find him. And if you've tried to find him and you haven't been able to, eventually you'll decide to stop your search and live with the fact you haven't been able to find him."

For a second I felt like I was twelve years old and we were on our way to the town hall in Someren. Once again I saw Anneke trying to shield me from disappointment. And for once I saw that she wasn't doing it to hurt me, but because she didn't want me to suffer any more than I already had.

"Maybe you think that looking for this boy brings you closer to your parents. Maybe he could tell you about the accident. But that won't change anything. It happened, your parents are gone, you're the survivor. Perhaps we should have talked about this long ago, but I didn't know how to, sweetie, we didn't know how. Jan and I also survived the accident, though we weren't there. It changed our lives, too."

I remembered the first time I saw Anneke and Jan in the hospital, and had asked myself why they were there, where they had come from. And the doctor's words: *Your parents couldn't come to see you*, a sentence that was far too long for expressing something that could have been said much more concisely.

"I would never have chosen this, sweetie. But now I know that I would never have wanted to be mother to any other little girl in the world than you."

Him

I didn't know whether to go searching or let myself be surprised.

I didn't sleep for a single second of the two hours that remained of that trip on the Talgo to Barcelona when I met Paco and his son Roberto. We arrived at the station and I bid my two travelling companions farewell. Paco was returning to Madrid on the Talgo that same evening.

Roberto told me that his next train left the following evening for Vigo and urged me once more to join him. I was so tired I couldn't think clearly. Perhaps that's why I agreed. Because I didn't have the faintest idea what I was saying. Or perhaps I thought it would help fill my empty days.

We agreed to meet in the station the following evening. I had thirty-six hours to kill. I called Simon and spent them at his house. After sleeping all night, I was overcome by doubts about whether I should board a train that would take me somewhere I had never set foot before. But I had an agreement with Roberto and I have always been a man of my word, so I put it out of my mind and the next day I showed up at Sants station, ready to go.

Roberto greeted me with a smile and I immediately felt I had made the right decision. He showed me to the only compartment that hadn't been booked that day. He set up a bunk and showed me how the bathroom worked just as if I were a paying passenger, reciting his instructions from memory. Before leaving to greet more passengers he told me to come to the restaurant car a few minutes after the train departed.

I was alone in the compartment, looking through the window at people rushing toward the train. By the time the train left the station, night had fallen. I looked around the compartment and realized that I would be spending the next few months in such a space.

I went to the restaurant car. Some of the tables were occupied, but Roberto hadn't arrived yet. I took a seat and waited.

"So, in the end you decided to go searching, instead of letting yourself be surprised," Roberto said as he sat down across from me. I said the first thing that came to mind.

"I boarded the train because I need to get my feet off the ground. I need to get away from myself."

Roberto looked at me steadily, while he processed what I had said. To me it had sounded empty and meaningless, but he had taken it to heart.

"You've come to the right place, then," he eventually said.

Though I didn't believe Roberto could really understand what I needed right then, a part of me wanted to believe that this trip to nowhere really could lead me toward a meaningful future.

I spent several months in the dark. Now, looking back, I know they were months, though at the time I had no idea,

I had lost all notion of time. I also had no idea I was in the dark, because I kept turning on the lights, but the problem was that there was no light that burned as brightly for me as Willemien had.

Over the course of seven months I slept in dozens of hotels, on Roberto's tab, or in hostels. The first few weeks I traveled only with Roberto, but I soon got to know the other conductors, and after a couple of months my dance card was full with trips from Barcelona to Vigo, from Madrid to Seville. Once in a while I got left on the platform when my conductor's car was fully booked by customers who had paid for their tickets, but fortunately that didn't happen very often.

As might have been expected, those first few nights were filled with monologues that I attempted to follow, until one day, after a few months of traveling, when Roberto asked a question that helped draw me out of myself. We had been on the train from Barcelona to Paris for several hours. The only thing I could think about was the first time I had been to the French capital, on my way to Holland.

We were in the restaurant car and we had exhausted several topics of conversation already when Roberto asked casually, "What was Willemien like?"

I thought he expected a few well-chosen adjectives, like attractive, gentle, intelligent. But while the words danced in my head I realized they were meaningless. They wouldn't set her apart from any other woman Roberto had ever met. I was lost in thought and Roberto apologized for his question, assuming I didn't want to answer.

In that second it seemed to me my heart became less heavy, that I could sit up straighter, that I could smile authentically. It was as if the day had suddenly brightened, and I realized the moment had arrived when I could finally talk about Willemien without grieving her absence. And I was eager to talk about her, I wanted to tell my young traveling companion all about her, and without knowing where to start I began talking before Roberto had another attack of logorrhea and I couldn't get a word in edgeways.

"Willemien never ceased to amaze me," I said. Roberto paid closer attention. "Willemien was constantly reinventing herself. When something had been in the same place for a long time, she would move it, to see how it affected everything else. When she had been doing something she loved for a long time, she would try something new, until she loved doing that, too." I had never tried to sum up Willemien, I had never stopped to think about what she was like, or how I saw her. But Roberto had prompted me to think about her differently, so I did my best. "You know what, Roberto? I probably chose Willemien because back then she was with someone else, and I needed to triumph over someone. I think she chose me precisely because I fought for her and won. Sometimes the reasons that two people come together are completely circumstantial. But all that matters is what happens next. And what happened was that we got to know each other, and since we came from different places there was a lot to get to know. I could tell you that what I liked best about her was that she was this or that. But the truth is that I liked her because she chose me. And that over time, despite everything, she continued to choose me day after day."

Roberto looked at me in awe, as if I were a wise professor and he were an eager student. I felt close to Willemien because everything I had been saying was something I had learned together with her.

"Of course, there were some surprises," I continued. "Things that reminded us how different we were, things that caused us to clash. But living in another country and adapting to another environment makes you humble and tolerant. And we both had that opportunity. First me in Holland, then her in Spain."

I looked around, the restaurant car was starting to fill with people, but it was so late at night that everybody seemed to be keeping quiet in deference to the distinctive clickety-clack of the train. Everyone murmured instead of talking, except Roberto and myself. We had lost all notions of circadian rhythm. We were more used to being awake at night than during the day; and we felt at home on the train.

"Love isn't what it used to be anymore," Roberto said despondently.

"Love, I don't know, Roberto. I think it's different for everyone. The only thing I know about is what my life with Willemien was like."

"How was it? Happy, right?"

"Yes, well, I could tell you it was an endless series of adventures we shared, of countless rough patches to get through, requiring innumerable gestures of goodwill."

"Adventures, rough patches, gestures," Roberto repeated, in an attempt to memorize three magic ingredients I had just revealed to him.

"Yes, I think so. Adventures, rough patches, and gestures, all floating in a vast ocean of routine."

We were looking out the window, but in reality we were looking inwards.

"Until the ocean dried up," I said, rising from the table. I realized I had said enough, and I wished Roberto a good evening and went off to bed.

A quarter of an hour later I was lying on the uncomfortable bunk in my compartment, thinking about lost opportunities, about how my life might have been if the ocean hadn't dried up. Recalling the future Willemien had planned for us.

One day long ago, Willemien had told me that we should take the money her parents had left her and open savings accounts for the children. Plus, she said, in a tone that was both cheery and determined, I would retire from work when I hit sixty and we'd be able to live without worrying about anything until we were one hundred. She had made out a budget based on two people living forty years. I remember the image that came to my mind, of two grandparents, shriveled as raisins, embracing in our bed one early fall morning, looking at the ceiling of our apartment in Figueres, deciding whether to walk down the promenade in Figueres or read the novel one of our grandchildren had written. I remember wanting to live with Willemien until we were two hundred. I said so, and then I said, *What if we don't die? What will we live on then?* and she began to laugh.

Now, after her death which was forty-four years too soon, and my retirement at the age of fifty-seven, thanks to her parents' bequest, instead of imagining two raisins looking at the ceiling of our bedroom I had to invent a new life for myself, to survive the endless years ahead, in which I'd have to live on the budget that Willemien had made for the both of us.

The night before I decided to stop riding the train I had a series of vivid dreams. I dreamed I was watching the stations pass by through my window, and at each station there was someone waiting for me, my children, my grandchildren, even Paco was waiting for me at one of the stations. But the train didn't stop. And I resigned myself to living on that moving train for the rest of my days. Until eventually, just when I stopped looking out the window, the train came to a halt. I looked outside and saw that I was at a deserted station. I gazed out the window, as far as I could see, looking for the silhouette of someone, anyone, Arjen, Simon, Robert, or Antonia, any of my sisters, I even looked for Pedro and Mariana. But there wasn't a soul waiting for me at the only station where the conductor of my train had decided to stop.

Yet something made me get off the train. No suitcase, no coat, I alighted at the deserted station.

I remember how the train doors shut behind me, the train gathering speed as it moved away from the station. At the same moment I saw millions of beams of light in front of me, as if I were a star scattering rays of light, as if I were my own giant light bulb. Each ray of light was distinct from the others, and each ray of light was one possible version of the future.

The next morning I awoke feeling at peace, I chose one of those rays of light I had seen in my dream, I said good-bye to Robert, and got off the train.

Her

Something broke inside me—as if all the pieces of an impossible jigsaw puzzle had finally been assembled and then they fell apart. It happened right after I bought the paper. I hadn't expected it.

It was Saturday, I had gotten up early and walked to the supermarket to do my weekly shop. I knew that Lianne Pérez-Horst's article was coming out that day and didn't want to miss the paper. After filling my shopping bag, I paid for the paper on my way out and walked a few meters along the street. I had thought I wouldn't flip through it until I got home, but I couldn't wait. In the middle of the sidewalk I set my bag down on the ground between my legs and opened the paper.

Beneath the title *Unlikely Search for an Angel* I read the story of a desperate little girl. My heart shrank. It couldn't be me. It couldn't be that I was still that little girl. I broke into a cold sweat.

Next to a long column there was a photo of a list of one hundred names. A worn piece of paper I had carried around for months, for years. It was mine, I knew it, but at the same time I didn't recognize it. In the photo in the paper my list looked like the scrap of paper a policeman finds in the pocket of a dead man, and which he keeps as evidence. Beneath the list there was a photo of Karen Abrams and me together in the bar. Karen Abrams was laughing, looking at the camera. I was looking sideways at the floor. My body looked tense, as if I were afraid, but I didn't remember feeling that way when she took the photo. I looked at my face carefully and I felt like I was losing my mind.

The images made the article seem unreal. I had become one of Lianne Pérez-Horst's characters, a confused little girl who had invented an angel and spent her life searching for a hologram.

I hadn't felt this way when I read the draft of her article. The photos and the newspaper had endowed the story with a fictitious quality. From the outside, this girl's life was so transparent. I was standing in the street, with my shopping bag between my legs, the newspaper open in front of me. I cracked.

I woke up in a hospital bed. Again. This time Anneke and Jan were next to my bed. I couldn't speak. I cried for three days without stopping. Anneke held me for three days straight. She cried with me and I felt her with me.

Back home I found my inbox full of messages Lianne Pérez-Horst had forwarded to me. Most of them expressing sympathy for that eight-year-old girl who had lost her parents. A number of them suggested I get in touch with the TV show *Disappeared*. Some of them recalled something about the accident, but no one knew anything about the man I had perhaps invented. Jasper Bouwmans, Ineke Crooijmans, Julie Martens, and Loesje Meijer, people on my list whom I had already found, wrote that they were thinking of me, and that they hoped the article would help me find my savior. I didn't receive a single message from any of the twenty-seven people I had yet to meet.

The days were suddenly empty. After a week at home I slowly began to return to my life, but in a new way. During the day I worked and I spent the rest of my time at home. The weekends were tricky, but Anneke often kept me company. She looked after me.

I didn't have anything to do. There *was* nothing to do. There was a huge void ahead of me and I didn't have the faintest idea of how to begin filling it. Sometimes Karen Abrams called from the bar, when it was quiet. She said she missed her best customer. Karen Abrams told me stories about the bar. Things her customers had told her or things that had happened in the neighborhood. At times I thought I'd be happy if I could have Karen Abrams's life. Or if I could share her life.

Life could be simpler than I had made it. But I didn't know where to begin.

One day Lianne Pérez-Horst came to see me. I came home from work to find her sitting with Anneke in my living room. I took a deep breath and smiled at them both while I took off my jacket. Anneke was sitting at one end of the sofa, like she didn't belong there, and I could tell from her face that she wasn't sure whether she had made the right decision, letting Lianne Pérez-Horst in.

Anneke offered to make some tea and went to hide in the kitchen. I sat down on the sofa, as far away as possible from the woman who had changed everything.

"How are you?" she asked gently.

"I'm fine."

"Have you heard anything?" she was talking to me as if I were unwell.

"You think I imagined my angel," I stated.

"No, that's not what I think. There's no way I could know. I wasn't there. You were."

I looked toward the kitchen. I missed having Anneke near me.

Lianne Pérez-Horst began walking around the living room, looking at everything like she was a detective. It was exactly what I had expected her to do, it was the reason why I had wanted to do the interview in Karen Abrams's bar, not at home. And after all that, here she was in my living room, looking at the photos of my past.

I closed my eyes and wished for her to stop, for her not to say anything else, and with my eyes closed it was like I could read her mind. I knew she was looking around, I knew she wanted to say something, although she didn't.

The photos on my wall were old. They were images of another time, another life. They were scraps of the life of an eight-year-old girl who no longer existed. None of the people in the photos were still alive. Maybe it was my fault. Because ever since my parents had died nothing had changed, despite the fact I was still alive; I had let life slip away.

There was no point in continuing to live that way. I opened my eyes and wondered whether one day I would hang a photo of Lianne Pérez-Horst on my wall. Whether she would play a role in my life beyond the one she had already played as a journalist. I imagined watching her children grow up, and, one day, seeing her soccer-fanatic son play for Ajax and thinking *I've known him since he was a kid.*

I felt the urge to open up to more people, but at the same time I repressed the urge to call Karen Abrams. I realized Lianne Pérez-Horst was, in a way, my savior. Her presence, her questions, and her behavior made me want to be different, to change things, to want to live my life.

"I have something for you," Lianne Pérez-Horst said when I had come out of my reverie. A month had passed since the publication of the article and she had brought a bag full of letters. She forwarded the emails as soon as she got them, but she hadn't had time to send the letters, she said.

She brought me the bag and set it at my feet.

"Have you opened them?"

"Of course not."

Anneke returned from the kitchen. I looked at her and realized that her presence at my side was completely unconditional. She had put up with everything and she was still there for me. She still believed in me. She still lived for me. I felt grateful for the fact that, after all I had done, she still wanted to be my mother.

"Lianne Pérez-Horst brought some letters for me," I told Anneke, handing her the heavy bag. I didn't know what else to do with the letters. I didn't know what to do with myself.

"We'll open them some other time, okay?" she said, taking the bag. I didn't reply.

It was quiet while she took the bag to my office, and it was still quiet when she returned.

"Are you still working through your list?" Lianne Pérez-Horst asked tentatively.

It was the first time since I had met her that she seemed unsure of herself. It made her more real, more fragile, made me feel closer to her. Could I be friends with her? Was there a place for her in my life?

"I gave up the search," I said. It was the first time I'd said it aloud. I still wasn't sure if it was true.

"Searching tires you out," Lianne Pérez-Horst said. "Sometimes we find what we're looking for as soon as we stop. I don't search, I find. It makes me feel good."

Maybe she was waiting for me to say what I thought, but I didn't say anything. Anneke nodded.

"I accept what comes my way," she added. "I let myself be surprised, but knowing that whatever happens to me, it's for the best, or at least something good will come of it."

It couldn't be true that everything in life just came to you. It also couldn't be true that whatever happens is for the best. Sometimes you have to search for happiness. And sometimes misfortune befalls you, you can't escape it. So it's better to search for happiness. To find the things that are important to you.

If I didn't search, there was just a void, a void I couldn't face.

There were ways to fill the void. If I gave up my search I could search for something else. I could concentrate on the word in the box, on finding out what it meant. It might be even more difficult than finding the people on my list, but I had never shied away from a challenge. And at the very least I would be filling the void, not just finding something.

There were other options, too. I could look for my cyclist. Spend my days looking for the man who had said I was *very nice*, to thank him. I could look for him near my office, posting flyers all over the city or riding my bike around town.

There had to be something. There had to be something more than getting up each morning to go to work, and eating dinner, sleeping, and going back to work the next day. How did other people do it? How did they survive without searching? How had my parents done it? Were they searching for something too? Or had they accepted the hand that life dealt them? The hand they had been dealt was death. I didn't want to wait until I died. If I was going to do that, it would be better to die right now.

I don't know how long I spent lost in thought, but I know that suddenly I felt Anneke's hand on my shoulder, and that my last words hung in the air. I'd rather die right now.

Lianne Pérez-Horst was looking at me, startled. Anneke was calmer, because it wasn't the first time she'd heard me say it. I was embarrassed to appear so disturbed. I sensed that Lianne Pérez-Horst would never be my friend, and I hoped that she would never write another article about me.

"I think it's a good idea, to end your search," Anneke said. "You've searched everywhere and no one has been able to confirm that this boy was real."

I recognized her careful tone of voice and knew what she would say next.

Lianne Pérez-Horst rubbed her hands nervously on her thighs. Anneke put a sentence together in her head. But I didn't give her a chance to say it.

"You both think that I imagined the angel," I said.

Lianne Pérez-Horst seemed like she was going to say something but she refrained. She looked at Anneke and Anneke looked at me, worried.

"It doesn't matter," I said, and I meant it. "Now I think so too."

Him

The day Willemien showed me her last artwork I didn't know whether to rejoice because it was nothing like emptying a bottle of lemonade into the sea or to pinch myself awake from an astonishing dream.

I wish I could recall the exact words she used before showing me something that was neither a painting nor a poster—it was nothing I could have imagined beforehand. But I now know I could never explain it as magically as she did to me.

Willemien stopped painting when she realized that art could be more than a reflection of my dreams, or the reflection of the landscapes of my homeland. For her, "more than" meant it could be artwork in and of itself. I had understood that much; we hadn't spoken about art for years, because we had been focused on bringing up our boys, getting settled in Figueres, and starting the painting school, which is where I thought she was getting her weekly dose of art, teaching her students. But there was more. Willemien had continued her exploration in silence, in secret. Until she decided it was time to include me in her journey, and its outcome.

It was a summer Sunday, we had gone for a walk after siesta and on the way home Willemien wanted to stop by the art school. She wanted to show me some of her students' paintings, she said. It had been a long time since she'd shown me one of her posters or constellations and, of course, it had been even longer since her last painting. Although we were going to see her students' work, I knew there was something else she wanted me to see.

When we entered the little school I rediscovered the scent of our attic in Eindhoven. That scent of oil paint, brushes, and imagination that was spilling down the stairs of our first house each time I came home from my light bulb factory. Accompanied by nostalgia, time lost and time gained.

With the passage of time, nothing is what it seems.

I paused on the threshold while Willemien turned on all the lights and chose some paintings to show me. Then I walked in. She showed me pictures of the sea, of forests, and of colors.

"These paintings are my students' attempts to recreate reality. Each time they're faced with a blank canvas they try to think of something they're familiar with or of an idea they have and they hope to capture on the empty space in front of them."

While she spoke, I was thinking of her students and wondering if they sometimes got lost listening to Willemien. I looked at the paintings, knowing that there was still some time before she would show me what she really wanted to. I wasn't sure whether she wanted to hear my opinion of these other people's paintings, or whether they were part of a journey I needed to take to prepare me for something else.

"Some are better than others," I said, trying to show some interest.

"They're all looking for something they won't find," she said solemnly. "And I won't find it either."

I've always thought it was that confidence, that conviction with which she pronounced things, which made it possible for her to create art.

She accompanied me to the smallest room in the school, the one she had initially used as a storeroom. I hadn't set foot in the room since we had opened the school, and Willemien had never told me she had turned the little room into her studio. She opened the door and I was surprised to find the space so different from how I recalled it. Instead of a dark, dirty storage space, we were in a twelve meter square room with a crystal-clear skylight in the roof and blinding white walls. In the room, which didn't smell like anything, there was nothing but a table and a small cabinet. There wasn't a single pencil or sheet of paper on the table, the table top was clean and empty.

The space seemed strange, otherworldly. I missed the chaos of our Dutch attic.

"This is the ideal space for creation," she whispered in my ear. "There's nothing here. Nothing to distract me from the essential."

"But there's not even any paper to sketch on," I said, bewildered.

"There used to be. I had pencils and sheets of paper. But they distracted me from what's essential. They made me draw pencils. So I put them away. Look."

I opened the cabinet and saw a shelf with paper, paintbrushes, pencils, and a few small paint cans. A tiny number of things, compared to the overflowing cupboards in the attic of our house in Eindhoven. This cabinet was more empty than full. Apart from the shelf with supplies, the shelf above held dozens of art books.

Eventually I looked at the bottom shelf of the cabinet. Near the floor there was a cardboard box full of burnt paper. I bent over to take a closer look. The side of the box said *constellations*. I was going to ask Willemien what was in the box, but she didn't let me. While she shut the doors of the cabinet she said, "I keep it closed, I don't take anything out until I've made some progress in my search for what's essential."

I didn't understand what she meant by *essential*, but I didn't ask.

"Art shouldn't represent," she explained. "It should be."

"Of course," I said. I had learned this lesson many years ago.

"When we look at something, as viewers we always ask ourselves what it represents, what it reminds us of. That's how we think we can understand a work of art."

I thought of the lemonade being poured out into the sea and what it might represent. Willemien continued explaining her view to me.

"But I believe works of art aren't meant to be understood, they're meant to be felt. And since our minds are always trying to understand things, we need a work of art that can't be understood at all. Something you can only feel. It's about making a piece of art that doesn't represent anything, and doesn't remind anyone of anything either."

"Can that be art?"

"Of course! Because it will move people. Do you see what I mean?"

She had lost me. I wished she would show me her painting, or whatever it was. Maybe she saw the impatience on my face. She asked me to leave the studio for a moment.

When I left the room I was confronted once again by the smell of paint I knew so well and that, in some way, I missed in her studio. For nearly a quarter of an hour I waited, pacing near the closed door and wondering how she had managed to keep the scent out of her studio.

I heard some sounds, as if she were moving the table or the cabinet inside the room.

"You can come in," she said, sounding far away.

I opened the door and from the threshold I could see the table was in the same place it had been before. The cabinet hadn't moved either. On top of the table there was a birchwood box that was no longer its original light color. Although it had been painted completely black, I recognized the jewelery box I had given her many years ago.

Willemien wasn't in the room. I went in and looked around. I wondered if she was hiding in the cabinet, but I remembered the shelves and realized she wouldn't fit. But I decided not to look for her. She wanted me to encounter that box alone.

I approached the table. There was a little key in front of the jewelery box. I tried to remember the last time I had seen the jewelery box, where it had been, what had been inside it. I couldn't remember. I took the key and put it into the lock. It opened easily. Before I lifted the lid I looked around me, listening, smelling. I felt like I was uncovering the secret of a stranger, like I didn't have the right to be there.

I lifted the lid of the box to discover an emptiness greater than that of the room I was standing in. At the bottom of the box there was an iron ring that made it look like the box had a false bottom. I put my finger in the ring and pulled carefully. I set the little panel aside and looked closely at what the secret compartment contained.

I saw a word. I tried to say it: "Breiszat."

But no sound came out of my mouth.

I was speechless, and my mind was blank. I just stood there looking at that word. I felt like smiling. As if I had just learned the secret of everything. And when I experienced this sensation, I wanted to share it with the whole world. I thought of all the people I knew, who ought to see what I was seeing, to feel what I was feeling.

When I'd had enough, I put the false panel with the iron ring back on top of the word, shut the lid, and locked it. Slowly I left the table.

Evening had turned into night. The skylight was dark, I had been standing in the shadows and I didn't know how long Willemien had been standing in the doorway, watching me.

"Did you like it?" she asked.

"Yes." There were some questions I wanted to ask her.

"Did you try to understand it or did you just feel it?" she asked, smiling.

"I didn't understand it at all. But I felt good."

"Then that means it works."

Her

Arjen Salgado was over forty, with tired eyes and a deep voice. We sat down on a bench in Vondelpark. He chose the bench. A few meters away, on another bench, there was a woman with a little boy. The boy must have been seven or eight and was pretending to make a toy plane fly, making different sounds. The woman glanced at us once in a while and shushed the boy when the plane noises became too loud.

Two days earlier I had received an email from Arjen Salgado. It didn't say anything about the article in the paper. He wanted to meet me to discuss something private, he said. It had been a month since I'd given up my search. I was certain his name wasn't on the list, but I still checked it to make sure Arjen Salgado's name didn't appear among the hundred.

When he arrived, I had already been waiting for him a short while. He sat down next to me on the bench, said good morning, and added, "My father died on a flight from Barcelona to Amsterdam."

I froze. I wanted to say *My father died on the road from Someren to Someren-Eind*. But I didn't. I realized that, suddenly, I had become the object of someone else's search.

He wants the box, I thought. But maybe not.

"I was there," I said to Arjen Salgado.

"That's what I thought."

"What do you want to know?"

For the first time he looked at me.

"I don't know what I want to know," he said, downcast.

I thought about the things I wanted to know about my parents. But it wasn't the same. I wanted to know why the accident happened, what made our car leave the highway and crash into a tree. I wanted to know if my father should have been driving more carefully, or if there was another car driving recklessly that forced our car off the road, or if an animal had crossed the highway, or if my parents had been arguing, or if the car was faulty, or if it had been sabotaged.

"He never liked to fly," he mumbled.

"Yes, he told me."

A group of skaters passed in front of us, they were fast. I looked at their legs, their feet, and the wheels beneath them. The woman on the other bench held the boy tightly in her arms. Arjen Salgado glanced at his wife and they smiled at each other.

"Why did you give the police someone else's business card?"

"I don't know." I tried to think of a reason. "Sometimes I do things without thinking."

There was a man sitting next to me who was looking at me because he knew I was the last person who had seen his father alive. And all I could say was that I didn't know why I did things sometimes. I wanted to be honest, despite the fact the things I did might seem strange indeed.

"I took a small box with me from the plane."

"Is that why you gave someone else's name?"

"No, the two things don't have anything to do with each other." But as I said this, I realized they might be related. He looked at me in surprise, almost angry.

"Don't try to tell me there's no connection between the fact that you stole something from a plane and then you gave someone else's name to the cabin crew."

"I didn't steal anything from Transavia." His surprise was turning into disbelief. "I didn't steal anything, I just took something with me." He was silent. "I talked to your father for a while on the flight. He told me about his life in Holland, his wife, Willemien, and their return to Spain."

When I said his mother's name, Arjen Salgado seemed suddenly to believe me.

"Your father was carrying a small wooden box. He told me that the time had come to show his sons some things. That he didn't want to wait any longer and run the risk of not being able to explain them."

"Why did you take it if you knew it was meant for me?"

"Because I had spoken with him."

"I want to see it."

"And I want to give it to you."

"Here comes the 'but'. . ."

"There's no 'but.' I'm going to give it to you."

"Have you opened it?"

"Yes."

"Why?"

"I don't know."

"Do you live nearby?"

"A quarter of an hour by bike."

"I want you to give me the box now."

I knew he was going to say that. Still, I didn't like the idea of giving up the box.

"We brought our car. I'm parked over on Amstelveenseweg. We can drive to your place and you can give me the box."

"I'll take my bike."

"We can put your bike on the car. I have a bike rack."

"Sorry, I'd rather ride my bicycle. You take the car. We'll meet at my place."

I gave him my address and told him how to get there. He said he didn't need my directions because he had a GPS. I walked to my bicycle and he went over to his wife and son.

On the way home I passed Karen Abrams's street. For a second I wanted to tell her what was happening, to get her to come to my house, too. I stopped in front of the bar, propped my bicycle against the window, and hurried in. Karen Abrams was behind the bar. The place was quiet and I decided there was no reason she couldn't come.

I was still a few meters away from the bar when I said, "Can you get away from here for an hour or so?"

"No," she said, without hesitating.

"It's important, you have to come with me. I found the dead guy's son. He's coming over to my place right now to get the box. I'm in a hurry. You have to come with me right now."

I had forgotten to breathe. I felt like a different person somehow. As if I wasn't the one in a hurry. Karen Abrams looked at me as if I were a different person.

She opened her mouth to speak but I wasn't listening. I had turned my attention to the street, to make sure my bicycle was still propped against the window. I turned. The bike wasn't there.

"Shit! . . . Shit! Shit! Shit!" I rushed to the door and looked up and down the street, but my bike was gone. It had happened so quickly. I clenched my teeth, standing silently in the middle of the street. Karen Abrams came over.

"What's wrong, cutie?"

"Shit. Karen. It's not my day. My bike was just stolen. I didn't lock it because I thought I'd only be in the bar for a second, but look, now I know that you can steal a bike in thirty seconds."

She put her hand on my shoulder.

"What can I do?"

"Not much, now. I have to run home, I have to get there before Arjen Salgado and his wife; if I don't, they'll think that I've tricked them. I just wanted you to be there, too."

"Give me a moment; I'll make some arrangements so I can come with you. I've got my bike but I can't give you a lift, we'll have to walk to your place together."

"Walk? We have to run!" I said, all worked up.

"Fine, we'll run! Wait a sec. I'll be right back."

I couldn't imagine Karen Abrams running. It didn't suit her. This was the first time I had seen her outside. In my mind she was always inside. Behind the bar, in her living room, in my living room. Never outdoors. But it turned out she also went outside and she was going to run with me.

A car pulled up beside me. The window rolled down and I recognized Arjen Salgado's wife's face. I was taken aback, and she noticed.

"Hey." Her expression said she didn't trust me.

"Someone just stole my bike," I said to convince her that I wasn't trying to run away. Arjen Salgado leaned over his wife's skirt, to get a good look at my face.

"Then hop in the car," he said. "We'll give you a ride." The thought of even touching the car paralyzed me. My feet felt like stone. Like the street had melted and my feet had sunk into the red asphalt of the bike lane; like I was at the beach, with my naked feet sinking into the sand as the waves came in.

I looked at the ground and suddenly Karen Abrams was next to me.

"Shall we?" she said hastily.

I couldn't respond. I couldn't breathe. I was at a crossroads, and the choice I made seemed to be one that would be final. It was my last opportunity to get in a car. If I didn't get in now, I never would again.

"Shall we?" Karen Abrams said once more.

Arjen Salgado got out of the car and extended his hand to Karen Abrams, announcing his name loudly and clearly.

"Karen Abrams," she said.

"We have to go now," he said, opening the rear door for me. I heard Arjen Salgado's son in the back seat, playing with his plane.

Time stood still. Karen Abrams waited for me to say or do something; Arjen Salgado held the door open, waiting for me to get in. I wished I would faint, to get out of the predicament. But I didn't. Karen Abrams came to my rescue.

"I'm going too," she said decisively.

"Why?" Arjen Salgado asked.

"Because she asked me to. And because I've seen the box, too. And because right now she's confused and she needs me. And because . . ."

"Fine. Let's go," Arjen Salgado said gesturing toward the car.

Karen Abrams didn't know that I had never ridden in a car since the accident. Maybe she thought I was frozen there because I didn't want to give up the box. Or maybe she thought I was afraid of cars. It didn't matter. Suddenly,

I came up with a solution. I could borrow Karen's bicycle. And she could go in the car. I explained my idea, and with each word my feet felt like they were released from the soft, sticky asphalt. I felt relieved, safe, and I was about to take Karen's arm and enter the bar to get her bicycle when Arjen Salgado froze me to the spot again.

"Don't even think about it! You're not going anywhere." He was angry and had run out of patience. "We're going *now*, in *my* car, to *your* place."

The boy in the backseat had stopped making noises. The woman in the front seat got out of the car. Karen took my arm and whispered in my ear. "What's going on? Why are you acting like this?"

I mumbled, "I can't get in the car. I can't. You go with them. I'll give you my keys and you can give them the box."

"Oh, sweetie. That's not what they want. They want you to go. C'mon, I'll hold your hand the whole way, I promise."

Karen put her hand on my back, caressed my cheek, and guided me to the car; I felt my body moving with her. First I put one leg in the car, I bent over to duck in, I perched on the edge of the seat, I lifted my right foot off the ground and all of a sudden I was sitting in the car. I scooted over to the middle of the seat, next to the boy. Karen sat beside me and shut the door gently. Arjen Salgado and his wife got in the car and shut the doors.

I was surrounded by people who were surrounded by a car. I tried to think about the people, not about the car. The son of a Spanish immigrant was driving silently next to his wife. The grandson of a dead man looked at me while he flew his toy plane. The first woman on my list of one hundred people stroked my hand softly. It was quiet. Dead quiet. I felt far away from the street and everything outside the car. It was quieter than a train or a plane. If I shut my eyes I could imagine I was in a movie theater, not a car.

When I opened my eyes again a few minutes later, my fear seemed to be gone. I wanted to call Anneke and Jan to tell them that I was in a car. I wanted to thank Arjen Salgado. I wanted to thank Karen. But I didn't say anything.

We got to my house. I got out of the car and waited for Arjen Salgado's wife to get their son out. I felt the warmth of the spring sunshine on my face.

I wished I could tell the dead man, Señor Salgado, that I had overcome my fear of cars thanks to him. Perhaps that was the reason we had been destined to meet. Perhaps Arjen Salgado was an angel, like the one I had been seeking for so long.

FINIS

To write the chapters about Him, I researched Spanish emigration during the 1960s and 1970s. My most important sources were the book *Ik kwam met een koffer van karton**, by the Dutch anthropologist Geertje van Os, and the website emigracioneindhoven.dse.nl, run by Miguel Ángel Luengo Tarrero, the son of emigrants. Without their work, I would not have been able to write this book.

Some of the situations in this book were inspired by the experiences of Spanish emigrants in Holland. All the characters are fictional, except one: Father Driessen. The Spanish emigrants in Someren held him in high regard and I have described him just as I imagined he would have conducted himself during the period. I hope I have done so accurately.

---

* Geertje van Os, *Ik kwam met een koffer van karton; Spanjaarden in Zuidoost-Brabant, 1961-2006*, Alphen aan de Maas, Uitgeverij Veerhuis, 2006.

Spanish translation: *Me vine con una maleta de cartón y madera. Emigrantes españoles en el sureste de Holanda, 1961-2006*, Cáceres, Junta de Extremadura. Consejería de Cultura y Turismo, Museo de Cáceres, part of the series "Memorias", 2009. (Author's Note)

ABOUT THE AUTHOR

LAIA FÀBREGAS (Barcelona, 1973) has a degree in Fine Arts from the Universitat de Barcelona. She has published three novels that have been translated to several languages. Since February 2012, she teaches creative writing at the writing school Laboratori de Lletres in Barcelona.

ABOUT THE TRANSLATOR

SAMANTHA SCHNEE's translation of Mexican author Carmen Boullosa's *Texas: The Great Theft* (Deep Vellum, 2014) was long-listed for the International Dublin Literary Award, short-listed for the PEN America Translation Prize, and won the Typographical Era Translation Award. She won the 2015 Gulf Coast Prize in Translation for her excerpt of Carmen Boullosa's *The Conspiracy of the Romantics*, which will be published by Deep Vellum in 2017. She is the founding editor of Words Without Borders and currently edits "In Other Words," the biannual journal of the British Centre for Literary Translation and Writers' Centre Norwich. She is also a trustee of English PEN, where she chairs the Writers in Translation committee. Born in Scotland and raised in Texas, she lives in London with her husband and three sons.